Son of the Circus
A Victorian Story

E.L. NORRY

Series
Tony
SCHOLASTIC

For my own unique rag-tag circus family:
Ed, Samuel and Maisy.

Published in the UK by Scholastic Children's Books, 2019.
Euston House, 24 Eversholt Street, London NW1 1DB
A division of Scholastic Limited

London ~ New York ~ Toronto ~ Sydney ~ Auckland
Mexico City ~ New Delhi ~ Hong Kong

SCHOLASTIC and associated logos are trademarks and/or registered trademarks of Scholastic Inc.

Text © E.L. Norry, 2019
Cover illustration © Alette Straathof, 2019
Poster p201 © Leeds Library and Information Service

The right of E.L. Norry to be identified as the author of
this work respectively has been asserted by her in accordance with the
Copyright, Designs and Patents Act, 1988.

ISBN 978 1407 19141 6

Printed and bound by CPI Group (UK) Ltd, Croydon, CR0 4YY
Papers used by Scholastic Children's Books are made from wood grown in sustainable forests.

2 4 6 8 10 9 7 5 3 1

www.scholastic.co.uk

PROLOGUE

Tell your neighbours! Tell your friends!
Fanque's show is here!
A circus so enthralling
All your cares will disappear

Edwin, Sid and Hugo
Defy Sir Isaac's laws
Their airborne antics always raise
Tumultuous applause

Brown the Clown turns upside down
All notions of decorum
His capers so comedic
Only strong ribs can endure 'em

Larkin the equestrian
Brings man and horse in chorus
With preternatural elegance,
A modern-day Centaurus!

The show that Pablo treats you to
Surpasses childish fun,
With wondrous tricks, you'll be transfixed
The moment it's begun.

1.

March 1867, Bradfield, South Yorkshire

I was twelve years old when I joined the circus.

One cold afternoon, Mother called me and my older brother George in from the street, where we'd been running along the tops of the walls between houses and the alleys, chasing each other.

George could never catch me; I ran too fast and was sure of my footing – even though the walls were high – and George always looked down, worried about stumbling over loose bricks.

I thought Mother meant to scold George again for not being wrapped up warm enough, but when we burst through the door, there was a man sitting with his back to us in the high-backed chair reserved for guests. His hat was on the hook inside the door and Mother's good china was upon the table, which meant he was important. Maybe she'd found a lodger at last. We needed one to bring in extra money.

I licked my fingers and quickly smoothed down the hair around my ears that tended to frizz up and out.

"Where is the lad then?"

The man's low, rumbling tone reminded me of factory machinery.

George threw me a what-have-you-done-now glare. I shrugged – nothing that I could think of.

We boys had no occasion for visitors. The only folk who came out to Bradfield, away from the bustle of town, were customers dropping off or collecting the clothes Mother mended for them. We weren't the poorest, but we rarely had meat with dinner anymore. Life had been especially tough since the great flood three years ago. We lived with our grandparents but their house had half-washed away, so we'd needed to move into lodgings, and there were fewer shillings to go around.

As well as mending, Mother now also worked five nights a week over at the Bull and Yoke pub that Grandmother ran. Neither of them smiled much these days.

"Boys!" Mother ushered us in front of the gentleman. The small fire behind us crackled, warming the back of my legs.

I'd never met anyone else with brown skin the same as mine and George's before, not unless it could be rubbed off – like someone who'd come out of the coal factories, or a chimney sweep's boy, covered head to toe in soot. But this man was darker than us both, and, somehow, the way he sat so upright and still made me think he wasn't ever teased about not scrubbing himself hard enough.

I stepped towards him.

He was a smartly dressed in a black waistcoat and dark grey-striped trousers. He slowly removed his tan leather gloves. Out of his waistcoat pocket dangled a gold chain, linked to a watch, which he was staring at, as shiny as any I'd seen. His moustache was big and bushy, and his hair fluffy, like mine. Didn't look like he went hungry, either, with such plump cheeks.

He smiled at both of us, though – his dark, lively eyes fixed on me.

"Come closer, both of you. I shan't bite."

If he was not a prospective lodger, perhaps he had come to offer me an apprenticeship? Mother had mentioned that the local book-binder enquired about me a few weeks ago – was this he? I'd been hoping for decent work, something less dangerous than the steel factory. Leaning over a grinding wheel, shaping steel knives and forks was hard, dirty work, and after George got particles in his left eye, leaving him partially blind, and developed a terrible cough, Mother stopped us working there.

"Edward," Mother said, sounding stern. "Edward and George, this is ... well, this is William Darby the circus owner: your father." She didn't look at us but lifted her chin proudly.

The silence was big enough to fall into. This man was our *father*?

Sometimes, in the dead of night, George and I played guessing games about who, and where, our father might be – George fancied him to be a sailor, and I an inventor, but we only span such tales to amuse and comfort each other. We had no idea who he really was. If we ever asked, Mother became upset. She said we were too young to know the details and that life 'was complicated' when a white woman chose to marry a man of colour. She told us that although some people were tolerant, her parents had refused to embrace him into the family because they disapproved of his profession – his class – as much as, or more than, his skin colour. But now here he was – a circus man?

Even though a thousand questions fizzed on my tongue, I waited quietly, staring at my grimy nails with my hands folded, knowing Mother would not appreciate me asking questions.

"William and I met some years ago, at his circus. I … I used to ride horses."

"And very talented she was too!" the man added, beaming.

I tried to imagine Mother on a horse. She had never mentioned such a thing! How could she ride with such big skirts and petticoats? Mother and Mr Darby smiled at each other and her eyes misted over. I poked George in the ribs, and he nudged me back, chewing his lip as if he was about to laugh.

She cleared her throat. "But riding horses and being on the road with two children became difficult, so we moved to live with your grandmother. Now, Pablo's troupe is touring around here, and he has … stopped by."

Was she blushing?

The man stood and bowed, with a flourish of his hand, twirling his fingertips. "Pablo is my stage name. Pablo Fanque." He smirked, though his quirked lip was aimed more towards my mother than us. "Fancier than William, eh?"

What foreign-sounding name was this? I had heard of the famous circuses of the day, such as Banister and West's, but had never heard of Pablo Fanque.

"Is Pablo a real name?" I muttered.

Mother's cheeks reddened and she gave a look that

told me I would be admonished once our guest had left.

"As real as Edward and George!" He roared with laughter, revealing his teeth.

"Are you married?" I blurted, unable to stop myself.

Mother's eyes went wide, and her hand flew to her mouth. If I was already in trouble, I may as well continue. I glanced at George – was he going to speak up? No, he just stared at the flagstones as if they held secrets he desperately wanted to discover.

William – for I was not about to think of him as Pablo! – roared his deep laugh again. "We are indeed."

Was laughing like a clown all this man did? I failed to see what was so amusing.

"Edward!" my mother said. "Don't be impertinent. The day your father has come to visit is very special. It's a day we should celebrate." Mother beamed at William, but she looked a little as if she might cry.

"You have met Pablo before, Ted. Do you not remember? You were very small. Perhaps three or four?" She sniffed.

I frowned. I had no memory of ever seeing this man. I sneaked another glance at George. There was no recognition on his face either. No doubt we were thinking the same thought: if meeting him was so special, then why had he left us in the first place?

He was clearly much older than Mother too; he

looked more grandfather than father.

I narrowed my eyes, deciding not to trust him. A man so old who had lured my mother away from her family to ride horses? What respectable gentleman would behave in such a manner?

William dug deep into his waistcoat pocket. "Here." He brought out a small paper bag. "For you boys."

I took the bag and peered inside. "George!" I held it out to him. He poked his nose inside and sniffed but stayed silent. With his cough, it hurt him to speak much. Poor George. Even though he was the elder, I usually spoke for both of us.

"What are these?" I asked, wrinkling my nose.

"Sweets," William said. "These ones are called ... 'unclaimed babies', I believe." He chuckled.

What a grim name. Was he teasing us? I picked one out and rolled the soft, powder-dusted figure between my fingers, before tentatively putting it into my mouth. George did the same. As we chewed through the sweetness, William watched us, smiling and smiling. He put his thumbs in his waistcoat pockets and leaned back.

Did he think we were won over so easily?

How dare he go off on circus adventures, leaving us to struggle? We could barely afford coal. The fact that we were mixed race with no man around the house to defend Mother's honour set the neighbours' tongues wagging enough as it was! Poor Mother worked herself to exhaustion taking in laundry and mending to support us and now that he was here, were we supposed to be overjoyed? Did he expect a fanfare?

Perhaps he *was* my father in name, but I had no need of this man in my life. I'd done fine up until now. George and I knew our friends' fathers and didn't think much of them, working in the mill or steel works but then spending their free time stumbling around from inn to inn, ordering everyone around, or, worse still, whipping them.

Mother said quietly, "Edward, as you know, we've discussed finding you a new apprenticeship. Since none is forthcoming, it has been decided that you are to accompany your father and learn the ways of the circus. George will remain with me until he grows strong enough to join you."

I coughed, nearly choking on my sweet. She was sending me away with this stranger? Father or not, she had not mentioned this possibility before. Although I hadn't attended night school in many months, I studied when I could. I wanted to better myself and was certain I'd find an apprenticeship soon. But was I expected to abandon my books and hopes simply to attend to this man?

George gave me a small smile, but his eyes looked sad.

I started breathing hard, remembering my only visit to the circus. I never wanted to experience it again. That hot July night at Aston Park had given me nightmares for months. George hadn't witnessed the woman fall to her death from the tightrope, but I had. After all the panic and screaming, I'd begged Mother that we never return. Although she seemed dismayed, she'd kept her word.

Until now.

I had to let this man know that I was no performer. "There's nothing I can do," I said archly.

William's voice boomed. "The horses, my boy. Riding horses will be in your blood. Both your mother and I have a talent for it. Trust me."

I'd rather not!

"I can't ride horses!" I cried.

I *hated* horses! Every time those huge stinking beasts trotted too near to me in the streets, I shied away. We'd never owned one for they were expensive to keep, and for that I was glad.

"You'll be light on your feet. I look forward to seeing you and the horses getting to know one another." William patted me on the shoulder. "You'll learn. I've worked with the biggest names: Young Hernandez and Jem Mace. I learnt from the best, toured with the best, and now ... well now, I *am* the best. I'll teach you."

Modesty was clearly in short supply at his circus.

"Are you ready then? To experience the adventure with me?" He sounded in good spirits.

This very moment? Mother must have noticed my panicked expression because she put her arm around my shoulder and pulled me close.

"Ted, let us gather your things."

She only called me Ted in her most caring moments. "George, fetch Pablo some gingerbread." George bit his nails on his way to the kitchen.

I followed Mother upstairs to the room we all shared. Once we were behind the door, I exclaimed, "I do not *want* to go with that man!"

She didn't flinch at my temper, just quietly collected an old cotton flour sack, my cap, two shirts and woollen trousers from the wooden drawers.

"Those trousers are George's."

"He's too big for them now. You may have them."

Mother sat on my lumpy bed and straightened the worn blanket. Seeing her hands so red and raw made me sad, but I still didn't want George's trousers! I didn't want to go anywhere – I wanted to stay here.

"In this life, there are many things we may not wish to do, and yet they must be done, all the same. Often, they reveal a life we've never seen. Do you understand, Ted? New experiences can be the making of us."

"I won't go!" I stamped my foot. "I want to stay here. Who will help George?"

"I will," she answered. "Pablo has given me five pounds. Now I can buy George medicine. We can travel if we need to. It'll be easier to travel around if I've only two of us to clothe and feed, Ted."

"W-will I see you again?" I stammered, staring at the floorboards. I couldn't bear to look into her deep brown eyes, usually so kind and wise. "Perhaps I will be more prepared ... after staying here one more night?" I asked, hopefully.

She smiled, but I knew her mind was made up because she stood up, smoothed down her dress and patted her bun back into place.

"I understand that this is a shock, Ted, and somewhat ... unexpected. When you were younger, your father and I agreed it was best for him to pursue his livelihood in the circus rather than struggle to forge a living here. You'll only be away a few months. Some things cannot be prepared for; they simply need to be experienced. Of course you'll see me again."

As if remembering her own circus life, her expression became dreamy. "A spring season, learning the trade and travelling, will be just the thing. You'll become strong and disciplined. Instead of burying your head in books, you will learn how to ride, tend the horses and earn your keep. And you will return to me a man."

Tenderly, she pressed the palm of her hand against my cheek. "I promise you, it will be a perfect adventure! My circus days were the happiest of my life. Now, if you've anything else you wish to take, best hurry along and pack it."

She kissed me on the forehead, sweeping out of the room with her skirts rustling.

From under the bed I grabbed my kaleidoscope (my most treasured special thing), tin soldiers, marbles and my issues of *Varney the Vampire*. All these I stuffed into the cloth sack. But remembering how George still liked the soldiers, I took them out and set them up in rows atop the drawers. Seeing them lined up reminded me I was leaving, and I became furious again. Just because circus days had been the happiest days of *her* life did not mean they would be mine! I belonged here with my family.

After a short time, I walked downstairs, my head and heart weighed down by what lay ahead. I did not want to leave, but my future had already been determined.

George was sat on the bottom step, twisting his cloth cap in his hands. I sat next to him, and I bumped his shoulder with mine. "I left the soldiers."

He looked sidelong at me. "You're to go off with that circus fellow then?"

George's cough may not have been severe enough to keep him from being packed off to the circus with me, but being half-blind in one eye certainly was. Only *I* would be leaving today.

He squinched up his eye, staring at the cap, now in his lap. "I shall miss you."

I put my arm around his shoulder. "I know."

"I'll ask Mother when we can visit."

"I wish you could come with me. Brothers together."

George sighed. "He only wants one of us. You, Ted. And why wouldn't he? *You're* in working order." He coughed hard, wincing. "Wish I was off to the circus."

He slowly walked up the stairs.

I stared after him sadly, wishing I could think of something funny to say, but my mind was as empty as my heart.

Clutching my cloth sack, I walked into the living room where William Darby, the circus owner, the father I had never met until today, was waiting to take me away.

2.

Once Pablo and I were out on the cold, now dark street, I asked, "Are we to get a carriage, Mr Darby?"

He laughed. "Call me Pablo. Please." He put on his top hat and disappeared around the corner. I followed him and his echoing laughs, my feet almost tripping over loose cobbles.

A massive black horse was tied up outside a closed butcher's shop. The beast had a thick glossy mane and its tail whipped back and forth. I shrank back; I liked to keep my distance from these creatures.

Pablo flapped his overcoat out and leapt up on to its back so smoothly that I blinked, not sure I'd even seen him move.

He extended his hand. "Come. We've a long ride to Raw Green." He sat proud in the saddle, looking a foot taller than he had in our cramped living room.

As I struggled, trying to get a hold on the horse,

half-balancing on a broken wheelbarrow, he yanked me up, frowning. "You've not ridden?"

I was embarrassed to meet his eye. "No," I admitted.

"You're too big to sit up front. Make sure you hold on to me though. We can't have you slipping off, eh, Ted?"

Had Mother told him to call me Ted?

It felt strange – too intimate – to be clinging round Pablo's waist, my cloth sack between us, as we sped through the streets. With my face pressed into his overcoat, all I could smell was hay and smoke. The wind sliced bitterly into my ears as our narrow quiet streets gave way to busier roads and we galloped past clopping carriages.

We were leaving home, leaving Bradfield behind, and I had no idea where we were headed or what kind of life awaited me.

Jostling about, I tried not to picture Mother and George settling down to supper. Questions thundered round my mind like the horse's hooves: where would I sleep, what would I eat, who would I meet, and what would this man have me do? When would I see Mother and George again? What about Grandfather and Grandmother?

The wind and cold air prickled at my eyes and I closed them tight against the soreness.

The longer we rode, the heavier my eyelids became, but I didn't dare doze for fear of falling. The tighter I held on, the warmer I became, and soon my numb fingers were forgotten.

Eventually, after riding for over an hour, we stopped. I wobbled, holding on to my sack, as Pablo helped me down on to the squelchy ground. All around was the stench of horse manure and wood smoke. The sky held no stars and was blacker than the mud at my feet.

"Where are we?" I asked.

"Raw Green, just outside Cawthorne," Pablo replied.

"A town?" I asked.

"No. We're a ways from Bradfield now, boy. We've set up in a good spot for a few days." He tied his horse up to a fence. I couldn't see much around me, but judging from the cold air, the sky free from factory smoke and the lack of noise, we were in a large open space.

I followed him to a small tent; glimmers of lamplight shone out from the crack at the front. Pablo pushed aside the canvas flap and directed me inside.

"Wait here. You must be hungry. I'll fetch you something to eat."

I sat on a narrow wooden bench and looked around, shivering. A gas lamp flickered. I shuffled my feet in the sawdust, looking off to one side where there were several wooden chests half-open with costumes, hats and feathers spilling out.

Pablo returned and handed me a cup of tea and a parcel wrapped in wax paper. Opening the parcel, I was thankful to see a hunk of bread, bacon and a piece of cheese. I took a bite of the cheese, which was rich and tangy.

Pablo stood watching me.

"Were your parents circus people?" I asked, between chews.

"No. My father was a butler, then a gardener, but I was orphaned."

"Have you not got brothers and sisters?"

He shook his head. "Not that I'm in contact with, though there were others. I'm the fifth son of John Darby. My father was from Africa."

"From Africa?"

"There have been Africans here since Roman times, though in Norwich, where I was born, I never saw too many fellows like myself."

"How did you end up here?" I took a long gulp of sweet tea.

"The family were in and out of St Andrew's workhouse. My mother had a daughter but she died. I was born in the workhouse three years later. The French war brought poverty for us working folk. Although the war ended in '15, there was much hardship. Parish officials could bind a child to a master—"

"—so they let you out of the workhouse to join the circus?"

"Oh, no. Apprenticeships needed to be respectable and the circus was considered anything but. I don't recall how I came to be apprenticed exactly. Perhaps it was a private arrangement between my father and William Batty."

As I swallowed my bread, washed down with tea, I thought over everything he'd just told me. How sad, growing up without his parents. I might not have known Pablo until today, but at least I had Mother and George. For a while, I chewed silently, imagining being as alone in the world as Pablo must have been. Had it felt like this, how I was feeling now?

It was very quiet, except for my chewing. "Where is everyone?"

"Sleeping. Most have lodgings in town."

I finished up my tea. My growling stomach settled as the bread, bacon and salty cheese filled it. What did I want to know most?

"What will you have me do?"

"You're Pablo Fanque's son! No need to sound so timid. I rope-walked at eleven. Though, in truth, my real passion was for the horses. I took to those animals as naturally as if they were people. Learnt to train them quick enough too. The circus runs through your blood! Dark and wild!" His eyes lit up.

I wasn't stirred by his enthusiasm. If he cared so much, why not come to fetch me and George years ago? Before we needed to work, and George had become half-blinded. A true gentleman would have put his family first.

I was here now, and although I had no choice, surely I could be more useful than learning silly circus tricks. "I've been to evening classes, I can read."

"Your mother said as much." Pablo plonked a muddy boot up on the bench, resting his elbow on his knee. "But it's time for you to be schooled in the ways of the circus. Learn to entertain. Crowds will marvel at how you balance and dance on a horse's back, just like they did for me. I'm not as young as I was, but the Fanque name can once again sing on everyone's lips."

He looked away and dusted down his trousers, picking at imaginary fluff. "My other boy left, struck out on his own."

I raised my eyebrows. "Your *other* boy?"

"My oldest son, Lionel." Pablo's face grew serious and his mouth turned down. "His mother ... died. A long while back. My circus has been missing that family connection ever since he decided to seek his fortune elsewhere." He smoothed his moustache and rubbed his chin.

I had *another* brother? "What happened to his mother?"

He stared at the ground, eyes dulled and dark. "She had a terrible accident. I think it was her death that caused Lionel to leave, to want to strike out on his own. This is all years before you were even born, Ted. But . . . life often gives you what you don't realize you need, and a few months after, I met Elizabeth, your mother."

He looked at me and that twinkle in his dark lively eyes was back. He was clearly a man who didn't stay dejected for long.

"How old is Lionel?" I asked.

"Oh, he'd be about thirty now." Pablo straightened his overcoat with a snap. "I don't want my circus to be without a son of mine. A family connection is important. I am determined that good times *will* return. Now, rest a while. I have urgent financial matters I must attend to."

Swooping his overcoat around him, he left.

I tightened my jacket around me, tired down to my bones. Only a few hours ago I'd been running, leaping over walls, with George. Now everything was different.

Pablo the circus man had another wife *and* another

son? What sort of man was he? And where was Lionel now? Pablo didn't want *me*, he just wanted any slave to teach his tricks to. He didn't really care! He'd been content to tear me away from Mother and George, who wasn't only my brother but my closest friend.

My throat closed up, as if it was being squeezed tight, and my eyes prickled with tears. I rubbed at them hard, blinking them away.

3.

The tent entrance flapped and a boy entered. He looked taller than me, though he was skinny. I'd never seen such long spindly arms and legs, like a marionette whose strings had been cut. He stepped forward and, somewhat fiercely, peered at me; his small eyes blacker than coal, with heavy thick brows, stared into my face. His skin was darker than mine, his lips thick and unsmiling. Pockmarks and tiny scars littered his cheeks.

In my twelve years, I'd not seen many people of colour, excepting my brother, but already today there had been Pablo *and* this boy!

He hawked spit into the sawdust. "You the new one?" His voice was low, almost a snarl. "The replacement for Lionel?"

I drew myself up and said indignantly, "I am the replacement for no one. I am Edward." Bold as I dared. Bolder than my quaking knees revealed.

I felt as if I'd been transported to another land. Maybe I *wasn't* alone after all. Maybe something good could come from belonging to the circus. But this boy didn't look like he wanted me to belong. He moved closer, loose and springy on his toes, almost readying for a fight. I shrank back.

"There ain't too many of us about, in case you ain't noticed." He indicated himself, sweeping his arm down from head to toe. "You're another of Pablo's sons then," he muttered, before spitting again. This wasn't a question.

"Yes, I am." I hadn't decided if this was a good or bad thing yet. My voice trembled, as I added quietly, "I have a brother, George, too."

"Where is this brother then? Quivering behind some petticoats?" He scuffed the sawdust at his feet.

My shoulders sank. "He isn't here. The circus has no use for him. He's at home with Mother."

"With Mother?!" he mocked, his voice high and strange.

I cleared my throat, trying to deepen my voice, which had not yet become a man's, to match his even, steady tones, but it came out like a whisper. "Are you Pablo's son too? Are we brothers?"

"Am I . . .?" The boy smirked, raised his eyebrows, and then dipped just one. "No. No. But he undoubtedly has been good to me." He glanced upward, thinking for a moment and sounded sincere as he added, "There are worse men to have as a father."

I wondered at this — what was worse than abandoning your wife and children?

"What's in there?" He lifted his chin towards the cloth sack at my feet.

"My things." I clutched the sack to my chest.

"Let me see." He didn't sound friendly. With one hand he rubbed at his short curly hair, smoothing it back off his forehead, and with his other hand he twirled something shiny between his fingers, over and over.

I held my sack tighter. What could I do if he came for it?

"Show me," he insisted, sitting next to me. Although he bumped me with a bony elbow, his voice was less demanding.

Reaching inside, I pulled out my kaleidoscope. Mother had brought it home for me after she'd been away, leaving George and me staying with our grandparents. She'd said, 'Be careful,' handing it to me. That was my clearest memory about receiving it, her instruction to be careful. I understood I'd been given a precious delicate object. Taking the wooden tube, I'd asked, 'What am I supposed to do?' and she'd laughed. 'Come over to the light and put your eye to it. Look through that hole, turn the tube around and tell me what you see.'

Lifting it, I had heard sounds like tinkling tiny pieces of broken glass, and I'd gasped at the shapes and colours that blurred and spun, intertwining, and then the coloured glass inside melded into different patterns, yet again! Glorious bursts of shapes like stars, clouds, or ink blots spreading across a jotter.

Now, this boy snatched it from my hand and held the bigger end up to his eye. He shook it. "This one of them picture tubes?"

I took it off him, gently, and turned it the right way before giving it back.

With his eye glued to it, he *oohed* and *ahhed*, and even though I was cold and grumpy, I let out my first laugh since arriving. "Haven't you seen one before?"

He rubbed at his nose. "Not for a long time," he said, handing it back. "Can't see much though. S'pose it's better in daylight?" He sounded hopeful.

"Yes. I'll show you again tomorrow, if you'd like," I said. He seemed a strange, complicated boy. Not quick to smile and please like George, or the others in our street. He was hot and cold. Was this what I was to expect from circus folk? It was unsettling, unpredictable.

"Show me your tricks!" he suddenly demanded.

"Tricks? I don't have any tricks," I replied, folding and unfolding my hands in my lap.

Springing up, he reached for the pole holding the tent up, and swung himself lightly around it, curling round like a snake. "No tricks!" he scoffed. "You can ride though?"

Unable to meet his bright blazing eyes, I shook my head, my cheeks flaming.

"Tumble? Spin?" His voice tore through me.

"No."

"Walk the rope? Juggle? Clown?"

"I cannot." Then I felt cross – as cross as I ever had. Just because I was forced to be here didn't mean I had to endure humiliation. Who was this boy anyway? "I can't do any of those things."

"Ha! You claim to be Pablo's son and you can't even flip?"

"I don't claim to be anyone!" I shouted.

This boy looked and sounded more like Pablo's son than me. I bunched my hands into fists. I didn't care; I didn't need either of them. They were welcome to each other! I felt a furious rush of heat, and my throat became thick and tight, and I couldn't swallow. Tears itched my eyes. That was twice now – me, a boy who never cried – feeling the threat of tears again on the same day.

I vowed to stay silent. If he wanted to carry on speaking, let him blather. I'd show him how dignified I was by my display of manners.

"What do they call you?" he barked. "Edward, you say?"

"Yes." Sulking was challenging when one was asked a direct question.

"Edward's too fancy a name for round here." He chewed my name over. "You need something shorter . . . snappier." His face brightened; he looked pleased with himself. "Eddie . . . Ed!"

"No." I wasn't going to have this circus boy name me. I sniffed haughtily, Mother's face swimming into my mind. "Call me Ted, then, if Edward isn't good enough for you."

He ignored my jibe. "Ted'll do nicely. I'm Larkin."

"Larkin? What do *you* do here?"

He laughed. The sound was rich and filled his body, reminding me of Pablo.

"What *don't* I do would be a better question! Used to sweep. Roads for a penny and then chimneys. They was a messy business; you'd get all scraped up from the insides. Pablo spied me carrying my brushes one day and he says, 'The law has changed. You shouldn't be sweeping now,' and I tells him since the cholera took my folks, I had to find my own way. He asks if I wanted to come along with him."

"How long ago was that?"

"About two years ago. First, I wondered what he

wanted with the likes of me, barely eleven. But now, thanks to him, there's not a tumble I can't turn, nor a horse I can't ride neither." His chest puffed out the tiniest bit.

Larkin was very free with what he was telling me. Were all circus folk like this? I wasn't quite sure what to make of it all. "I don't like horses," I whispered, the words out before I'd had a chance to think. Now he'd think me useless for certain.

Larkin barked a laugh. "Ha! Don't you worry about that. I know my horses, almost as well as Pablo, and I'm tasked with learning you."

"Teaching," I corrected.

He stuck his tongue out before grinning. "You'll be riding, not talkin'." He looked me up and down, taking me in. "We'll do balancing and stretching an' all, to build strength and flexibility."

"I only went to the circus once. A lady fell off the rope and . . . died," I mumbled, my eyes fixed on the ground. "It was the worst thing I ever saw."

"Well, that's what draws the crowds," Larkin said, lightly. His black eyes glittered, the dim light from the gas lamp throwing smudgy shadows against the canvas. "Not dying, but . . . the fact that any one of us *could* die. People pay hard-earned pennies to watch us do things they'd never dare. It's about . . ." He frowned, his

29

eyebrows knitting together, and I could see his mind trying hard to grasp the correct words, the meaning of what the circus meant to him. "…possibility, you know? The thrill that a lion *could* bite! Might. No one wants actual death, course they don't, but it's about feeling *alive*, in't it? People want … more."

"More what?" I breathed, taken with his passion.

He shrugged. "More than the dullness of their everyday lives."

As his words sank in, I bumped back to reality. Did people really want the *possibility* of death? I didn't think so. The screams at Aston Park had echoed through my mind for weeks afterwards.

I'd seen people taken ill before, and even men topple over drunk, but back then I was only seven, and in my short life I had never seen someone die.

When she fell to her death, I couldn't forget the sickening crunch as her body thudded to the ground, her eye bulging out, her skull no sturdier than a boiled cabbage. A hush rained upon us, before people rushed about screaming. We went outside with the rest of the crowd but I lost sight of George and Mother. Shoved to the ground, I ended up face down in a field, cold and crying for ten minutes, never knowing if I'd be found again.

"It's unnatural, standing on horses and walking on

ropes up high." I shuddered, remembering that evening and how terrified I'd been. "The circus is dangerous ... and, and foolish!"

"*Foolish* – it seems to me – is talking down your father's livelihood." Larkin picked at his fingernails. "It *can* be dangerous, that's true, but Pablo makes sure we're careful. Especially after..." He wiggled his eyebrows as if to indicate *I couldn't possibly say.*

"What?" I asked, not sure I wanted to know.

Larkin glanced around, although it was only the two of us. "Twenty years ago, his son Lionel was on the tightrope when the gallery collapsed. Hundreds of people fell right into the pit! His wife was taking tickets in the box below. She got crushed to death."

So *that's* what had happened! The accident Pablo had referred to.

"People say Lionel blamed Pablo for his ma dying, that it was Pablo's fault for reusing an old building. When Lionel ran off, it broke his father's heart – from the way Brown tells it. Pablo put ads in papers trying to find him, even offering a reward."

Why did Lionel blame his father? Whose fault was it?

"Anyway, with me instructing you, you've nothing to worry about. We begin training in the morning. By April, I'll have you vaulting over horses!"

I wished I could believe him.

4.

I wriggled, blinking hard against a beam of sunlight falling across my face. A heavy overcoat, which had been covering me, slipped to the ground. Feeble sensations from dreams of Mother, George and of sweet flute music came back to me, hazily. I could almost hear its strains on the wind now, like echoing memories.

So unsettled had my sleep been that it took me a moment to remember where I was: *the circus*. Unfamiliar and unwelcome, with no Mother and no George. Thinking of them having breakfast together, drinking warm sweet tea, made my throat dry and my feelings wobbly.

I'd fallen asleep in the small tent housing costumes and props. Larkin was nowhere to be seen. I sat up and rubbed my icy hands together to warm them.

The entrance was pinned back, and swirling dust motes flashed on rays of morning sun. Clear and crisp air rushed in, along with a small plump man. His coat was brown with a velvet collar, and a brassy-looking chain was draped across his sealskin vest.

"Welcome! Pablo said his son would be joining us. Wonderful!" He held out a chubby hand that I shyly took. He pumped my hand up and down so hard that I was sure my arm might come off.

"How did you sleep?" he asked. The man had short, light curly hair and his long face was flexible as dough.

I let go of his hand and rubbed at the small of my back, sore from the way I'd been lying on the bench. "Terribly!" I grumbled.

"I admit, the dressing tent *is* a funny place to take a nap! The sleeping tents are comfier, with blankets and mattresses."

"Why are we sleeping in tents at all – aren't circuses in buildings?" I stood and stretched. "That would be better than this!"

"Well . . . we're on rather a budget these days." He chuckled, but fidgeted awkwardly. "In the wintertime, if funds allow, yes, we may occupy a building. But Pablo doesn't like to use temporary ones, not after what happened, unless he's built it himself."

I said quietly, "Oh. The accident?"

"It happened in a temporary circus due for demolition. Pablo had taken it on at a budget price.

He wasn't to know that the beams had already been removed. The entire thing collapsed with all the people inside. Anyway, let's not dwell on such a tragedy. Now that the weather's becoming warmer, it's agreeable being outside." His eyes were hazel and kind and his manner gentle.

"It's a fine morning out there," he said, indicating the field through the tent gap. "About time you met our steeds if you're to be an equestrian like your father, eh? No time like the present."

Unable to meet his eye for fear of having him laugh at my question, I asked quietly, "Is he expecting me to do tricks immediately?"

"I doubt you'll be turning somersaults tomorrow, but you might have something to show us in a fortnight, especially with that famous Fanque blood flowing through your veins. Your mother was a fine rider too; it was quite something, watching her and your father perform."

I didn't want this stranger speaking of my mother. She wasn't a circus performer to me! She was mine, all mine — the woman who cooked me porridge in the morning and mended my socks at night and stroked my forehead when I was ill.

"Who are you?"

"Who am I?" Chuckling, he put his hands on his

hips, before looking around as if addressing a captive crowd. "Fancy the lad not knowing who I am!"

"I'm sorry." I straightened my clothes. "*Sir*," I added, in case he was important and I was being disrespectful.

"Don't you mind, boy. Nothing vexes me and I *am* out of costume. I'm Brown the Clown. A talking one mind you, not a tumblin' one. Come and meet the rest of the motley troupe."

The rest? I gulped, not sure I was ready to face everyone at once. Maybe I could keep Brown here talking for a while longer.

"Did you always want to be a clown?"

He smiled, lips stretching wide. "Oh no! I started off on the tightrope, but Pablo said I made him laugh so, and since one never knows what will tickle an audience, I started making up ditties and the next thing I knew, a clown I was! Come along – we don't want to keep Pablo waiting."

I rubbed my cheek where the bench had left grooves. I reached down for the overcoat and folded it slowly. My reticence must have been obvious because Brown said hastily, "There's not many here, just them lot who are always with us. They're friendly enough. Some might have airs and graces, that's only to be expected with *artistes*, but we're more like a family, I'd say. Other performers, the ones we hire in from adverts, stay in lodgings."

"How far are we from town?"

"Cawthorne's not too far, couple of miles. Come along."

I followed Brown out into the morning light. We trudged across a large open field surrounded by grasslands. Brown chattered, his sunny manner a marked contrast from Larkin's tempestuous nature. I could easily imagine Brown making crowds laugh.

"Pablo's quite the handy man. He built his living wagon himself to travel round the country. See?"

I looked across the grass to where six wagons were clustered. One of them had a roof and sides made from thin sheets of iron, like an enclosed trailer, built on a wagon frame. Was this considered luxury? How many weeks had Mother said I'd be here?

"That thing? Looks like a windowless box on wheels."

"A windowless box it may be, boy," Brown said sharply. "But with a sleeping area, heating stove and place to sit, it serves Pablo well enough. In the summer it becomes baking hot, so he prefers to sleep out under the stars. The rest of us sleep in the sleeping tents: one for the ladies and another for the men."

My stomach lurched. Even Brown must have heard

its grumble because he patted my arm. "Must fancy something to eat about now, eh? Let us fetch some breakfast."

A few hundred yards in front of us was another tent, at least ten times the size of the one we'd just left. This must be the circus tent. Although I didn't want to be here, I couldn't help but be impressed – it was twice as tall as our house! The thick canvas rippled and swayed with the wind, as if it had a life of its own and was taking a deep breath.

Brown rubbed his hands together. "Exciting, eh?"

I didn't want anyone getting the idea that I *wanted* to be here. If they thought that, I'd never be sent home. And that was all I really wanted – to be at home.

"I'm just . . . cold."

"Spring will be here soon enough. You wait and see. The daffodils are already making themselves known. There'll be bluebells before we know it."

A huddle of people stood near the large trailers that were in a circle, with boxes and trunks balanced on them, in the shade of the big tent. In the centre was a fire in an iron basket and a bubbling pot that smelled of cabbage and mutton.

People stared as we approached, and my cheeks

roared red. I turned to ask Brown something, but he'd gone! Everyone moved aside to reveal Pablo. He stroked his bushy moustache and came forward with his arms held out wide.

5.

"My boy!" He beamed and I felt warmer seeing his bright smile directed at me. "I doubt you got much sleep on that bench, eh? But you were in such a slumber I didn't wish to wake you, só instead I covered you with an overcoat. Now, you've met Brown the Clown." He pointed back towards the people by the wagons. "And that's Polly, Clara, Edwin and Hugo and Sid – they do acrobatics, juggling and riding, among other things. You'll get to know everyone as we go on. Now, though, I want you to meet my horses."

I tried not to stare at everyone, but I'd never seen such a variety of people before and my body hummed with the thrill of it! Maybe I wasn't so different after all.

Together, we walked towards the big tent.

Pablo cleared his throat and glanced sidelong at me. "You don't remember me, do you?" he asked.

"Should I, sir?"

"I told your mother that you wouldn't. A shame." He sighed, sounding disappointed. "We'll have to begin again."

With a flash, like a blast of a horn, I heard Mother's voice echoing from yesterday: 'You have met Pablo before, Ted. Do you not remember? You were very small. Perhaps three or four?'

And, out of nowhere, a memory shot into my mind, the same images that often troubled me in sleep: a man and me riding. Riding, riding, and explosions of thunder and BOOM! Banging on the cobbles: bang, bang and I'm jolted, needles of rain like scratches slashing my face. I'm bouncing, but it's not a carefree bounce, it's hard, and rough itchy cloth is squeezed against my cheek and it . . . *hurts*.

"Here we are," Pablo said, shaking me from my musing.

From inside, the circus tent seemed even bigger, if that was possible. Outside, it had looked vast, but inside was as spacious as a church.

A circular area was filled with sawdust, and benches lined around the outside. I tried to imagine the place as crowded and bustling as it had been on that terrible night at Aston Park.

"Impressive, isn't it?" Pablo mistook my paralysis for wonderment. "It's a pity you don't remember being here before, with me. You liked nothing more than to play in the sawdust with my pocket watch." He brought it out and waved it at me but I barely glanced at it.

I only remembered that of which I dare not speak: rattling cobbles and clattering hooves and banging and fear like I'd never known. My thoughts swirling and repeating: *Where am I? Where are we going? Where is Mother?* And then, the world tilted and I was falling, falling and scraping along the ground and bleeding before I was yanked, grabbed by my collar, nails digging into my neck, drawing blood, as I was pulled roughly up and slammed hard against something. The road?

He sighed and tucked his watch away. "That's the ring. The horses are stabled round the back, still inside the tent. Come."

I walked behind him, watching the way he swaggered, wondering if I'd be able to imitate his confident walk, or even if I'd want to.

What kind of man was my father? A man who had selfishly tried to save money by hiring a faulty circus building? Or a man scarred by a lonely childhood growing up in a workhouse? Being dark-skinned, did he feel alone and left out, as I often did? With the death of his first wife, and loss of his son, perhaps he'd tried to make a new family, but just found the lure of the circus life too strong? Was he all of these things?

I wasn't sure yet.

A section like a corridor had been roped off and these made up the stables, where the horses and ponies were divided up into makeshift stalls. Pablo stopped at a sectioned-off stall and ran his hands along the neck of a huge black horse that whinnied and stamped a hoof.

"This is Bessie. She brought us here last night. We've had a long and fruitful relationship, Bessie and I."

"They don't seem to have much space."

"Each stall is about three metres by three. Don't you worry; they can move around and lay down without restriction."

I lurched back when Bessie tossed her head. Her nostrils flared, steamy air shooting out. Pablo dug into his jacket pocket and brought out half a turnip. "Why don't you feed her, eh?" He held the turnip out to me.

And have that beast tear my hand off? No, thank you!

"You'd be better placed to feed her. She knows you."

He scrutinised me carefully, before laying the turnip on his palm. He lifted it towards Bessie's fleshy lips, which shuddered as she chomped down.

"We've eight horses and five ponies. I used to have more but those were . . . different times." Pablo stroked her mane. "It'll be Larkin who'll instruct you, with my participation. The trick with riding is balance. Balance and confidence. Trust and respect the horse and they'll afford you the same courtesy," he said.

Oh, was it that easy?

"That's the secret to riding, is it?" I couldn't help myself; I probably sounded impudent.

"There are no secrets, Ted. Eventually, the horse gains trust in the rider, and becomes used to whatever you introduce. Stroke first their neck, then the cheeks, and finally the forequarters. Never walk around the back, unless you want to risk a kick! Patience, understanding and … turnips. There is no other way with a horse, and never was. The most important thing – like with any animal – is kindness. They can be trained to do anything, *if* they're treated with kindness." He ruffled my hair. "Like sons."

Instinctively I jerked backwards, and his hand stopped mid-air. His mouth turned down a little. Had I gone too far and made him angry? There was a long pause.

"Ted. I am grateful that you are here. I'm … looking forward to us performing together, eventually. My son."

The word 'son' weaved its way into my heart. I let it sit there a while, seeing how it settled. Surprisingly,

45

it didn't feel stuck in my craw at this moment. Instead, the word 'son' seemed more like a stone that had been warmed all day by the sun, and the residual heat spread through my chest, filling me up.

"Breathe in deep through your nose," Pablo said, placing his hand on my shoulder.

I inhaled deeply. The smell of manure, hay and sweat was so strong it turned my stomach.

"There's no animal that smells as good as a horse, you agree?"

I did *not*! But instead of saying this truth, I asked, "How long have you been riding?"

"Apprenticed to Batty's Circus when I was ten years old. Before that, I'd not ridden. Ha! He had me up on a horse quick. I first performed in the ring when I was eleven, the day after Christmas."

A faraway look swam into his eyes. "There's simply nothing that compares to being on a horse when she trusts you. You've seen horses at the circus before, haven't you?"

I'd seen them thunder round the ring fast enough to kill a man and had imagined being trampled under those hooves ... I'd barely been able to watch. But Pablo didn't want to hear this – I was his son and he wanted me to learn his trade. I would never be able to admit my fear and dislike of horses, or the circus. I decided to state a fact I admired, and to leave my own feelings to one side.

"The men balanced on horses as if their feet were glued fast."

He smiled knowingly. "No glue, or ropes. When a horse canters round, it's the sheer speed that keeps the rider upright. Stops us from falling off. I can pick up handkerchiefs from the ground while Bessie's at full speed. Larkin does headstands in the saddle. I've ridden astride two horses at the same time while playing a pipe! Do you know what I did in my youth, m'boy?" He leaned into me, nudging me gently with his shoulder, grinning.

"No, sir."

"I performed in Manchester in front of *three thousand people*, leapt on horseback over a coach placed lengthways, and taught the ponies to waltz too!" He gazed upwards as if remembering that exact moment. His voice was joyous. He truly loved this life. Just yesterday I hadn't wanted to know anything about the circus, but his passion was starting to sweep me along.

I asked, despite myself, "What does it feel like?"

"Why ... it's like nothing you've ever felt. Power and speed ... like you can do anything. Like that's all there is. There's no time to consider anything else. All you have, or will ever need, is all there in that one moment. Bliss."

Stepping away from Bessie, he pulled out his pocket watch. Rubbing a thumb across the burnished gold, he added softly, "My home is in the ring. I'm at peace there." Then the circus showman, all bluff and bluster, took centre stage again. "Bess here loves to dance. When the band plays, she'll trot, pull up her legs and dance along. It's a splendid sight!"

"Pablo?" I whispered.

"Yes?"

"I'm very hungry. And … I need to … *go*." I crossed my legs hard, and jiggled up and down a little.

"Oh!" He stood back, startled. "There's a bank of trees behind the tent you slept in. After, find Polly – she'll fetch you some tea, and bread and cheese."

6.

After I'd relieved myself, I crossed the field and tried to take everything in: the crisp morning air, the stony ground and dry grass crunching under my boots. This was my home now, for the next few months, whether I liked it or not. This was no dream, or mistake.

"Oi!"

I turned to see Larkin cartwheeling across the field until he was in front of me, upright and breathless, with a tint to his cheeks and his eyes so dark they were almost black, flashing and sparkling.

How did he throw himself through the air like that and land on his feet, time and time again? What went through his mind when he was upside down? Wasn't he worried about hurting himself? It wasn't natural!

He was showing off. Trying to show me everything he could do that I could not.

"Ready, Ted? We can start your training. You've

lots to learn. We'll begin by getting you used to the horses."

I threw up my hands, exasperated. "I have had nothing to eat yet!"

"Oh, fine," he grumbled. "S'pose we need our bellies filled before we start leaping about."

At the fire, I held my hands out for warmth. Polly sat on the steps of Pablo's wagon, her fingers nimbly weaving a needle and thread in and out of shiny material that was in her lap. She was tall and thin, with dark hair coiled atop her head, like a length of rope. She looked older than us, maybe sixteen or seventeen.

"Pol, be a dear," Larkin wheedled. "Can we trouble you to get us some … provisions?" From the way he chewed on his lower lip and couldn't quite meet her eye, it was obvious he was sweet on her. George had started to act like this around a girl who lived down our road; I recognized the signs.

She glanced up at him and peered down her nose. "I'll fetch you some tea, but what are you gonna do for me, Master Larkin? You know very well that I'm still waiting on that shilling from last Sunday!"

"I'll pay you back, I will," Larkin crowed, dancing away from her outstretched palm over to me. "Met the newest member?" He grabbed my sleeve, tugging me forward, and I stumbled.

50

Polly set down her sewing and she nodded. "Pablo's son." She smiled kindly, her cheeks bunching up into two apples.

"Yes, m-ma'am," I stuttered. Whenever George and I had attended Sunday school we didn't sit with the girls, and there hadn't been any in our section of the factory, so I hadn't had much occasion to speak with many young ladies, certainly none as pretty as this one. Her eyes were the bluest blue; a striking combination with such dark tresses.

She burst into sweet-sounding laughter before leaning forward to pat me on the shoulder. "*Ma'am*? Oh, I like that! Larkin – you'd be best placed to listen to this gentleman's manners, he could learn you a thing or two! Here, have this." She handed me a lump of bread. "I'll make tea and fetch some more food." She left her material on the wagon steps and strolled across the field towards the smaller tent.

"What happens now?" I asked, watching Larkin's eyes follow Polly.

"We eat, dummy," he muttered, clearly not listening.

"I mean *today*. What do we do?"

"Mornings is rehearsal time. Those are the Bellini brothers over there. Learn from them while you fill your belly and then we'll get to them horses. I'll grab

51

the grub from Pol, you wait here."

I sat on the wagon steps Polly had vacated. The three men Pablo had mentioned earlier – Edwin, Hugo and Sid – were now all barefoot, wearing navy one-pieces. They threw each other around, looking loose and bendy, as if they were connected to each other by rubber bands.

Were these tricks Pablo thought *I* would be able to do? Because there wasn't a chance of that.

After the brothers had finished bouncing and throwing each other, they stopped and took a breath. They looked very much alike: short and stocky with expressive hands and animated faces, all with handlebar moustaches. It was difficult to tell their age; they could have been fifteen or twenty-five.

I walked over to them. "How did you become so skilled?" I asked in awe.

"We put in a good many hours practising."

"Rehearsals from six o'clock, all morning, every day."

"We've no other interest apart from whether Sid has learnt his double somersault on and off the pony, or whether Hugo should learn how to dance on the tightrope."

I was becoming dizzy, having to turn my head to follow their rapid flow of conversation as they spoke over each other; it was impossible to tell which words came from whom.

That had to be Edwin speaking then. "But how do you balance on one another at all?"

They had thick accents. I couldn't tell where they were from.

"You need to consider balance and counterbalance to achieve the variety of moves and lifts."

They spoke quickly. "One person might lift and support the other, or maybe even throw and catch them."

They smiled round at each other, and one clapped another on the back. They all seemed in perfect harmony with one another; happy, and at ease. Would I ever become this comfortable in my own skin?

Larkin trotted across to me carrying two large bowls. I grinned, seeing steam rising off them, catching the same mutton smell that I had earlier. Perhaps it was a little early for such a heavy meal, but I wasn't going to complain.

"Here," he said, thrusting a bowl into my hands. "The brothers are good, aren't they? They've been doing this since they were five years old, in Russia or somewhere. The more you practise, the better you get."

"Can you juggle?" one of the brothers asked me, his blue eyes sparkling.

I blew across the top of the steaming bowl I held.

"I can't do anything." I had the feeling I'd become familiar with hearing myself say this. Here, it seemed the things I *could* do – read fluently, help Mother bake, and dash along neighbours' walls whilst avoiding their outhouses – wouldn't serve me too well, now that I was a circus boy.

Edwin chortled. "If you've a mind to learn, there's nothing that can't be done. I started with juggling. The basic move is easy enough; make the objects follow each other in a circle—"

"—but then there's crossing," Sid interjected, raising his eyebrows.

"What's that?" I asked, slurping a mouthful of the thick, salty stew, full of watercress.

"That's not so simple. It's when objects are thrown alternately by both hands and cross each other in mid-air."

"Sounds impossible!" I said, between mouthfuls.

"No such thing!" Hugo climbed up on to Edwin's shoulders, to a standing position. "Sid, you've finished eating. Throw me those potatoes."

Sid took two potatoes off the plate at his feet. He threw them to Hugo, who juggled with them before Sid threw him another one.

"How are you doing that?" I coughed on a stray

leaf of watercress.

Hugo kept talking whilst juggling three potatoes, so focused and fluent. "Maybe you start with a balled-up bit of paper. Then you'd throw it from one hand to the other, gradually increasing the height and speed. Show the boy!"

Larkin put his bowl down on the ground. Larkin and Sid demonstrated with another potato, making it look effortless.

"Hugo!" Edwin yelped, suddenly rubbing at his shoulder. "Ow! Did you cut your toenails?"

Hugo laughed and jumped down, still juggling, until Sid swiped all the potatoes to the ground. "Aha!"

"And the tumbling?" I asked. "How do you start?" Perhaps I might learn something simpler; *anything* rather than having to ride horses.

"Handsprings, or flip-flaps, is basic tumbling. A handspring, Larkin!"

Larkin threw himself around us in a circle as the Bellinis once again talked me through their various moves and training methods.

"You fling your body forward on to your hands. Then your legs are thrown up over your body," Hugo explained.

Edwin added, "A flip-flap is the same move, but

done backwards. Somersaults? You can do them balled-up, arms hugging your knees to the chest—"

"—or laid-out with your body and legs extended," Sid chimed in.

Larkin stopped, out of breath. He smirked. "Fancy doing them tricks on a horse, do you, Ted? You're nothing if not ambitious! Pablo *will* be pleased."

I glared at him – not sure if he was mocking me.

Edwin said, "Boys! We've costumes to prepare. Come!"

The three of them sprinted across the field and around the back of the big circus tent.

Polly emerged out of the costume tent. It seemed like she was looking for something, searching about in the grass.

Larkin had perched himself against the wagon, munching the remains of his stew, watching her. "Polly is a fine girl."

"She certainly makes a good stew," I said.

"She's good at everything," he sighed dreamily, mopping up the last of his juice with his bread.

I had no interest in hearing him mooning. "Will we stay here long, at this ground?"

"Probably two or three days," Larkin explained. "That's usual. Has Pablo not explained how his circus works?"

"Not yet."

"He's leaving it to me then. I s'pose he has business to drum up. Coin to find, since it's scarce. There are two shows a day; one in the afternoon, about two, then we eat and rest till the next show around seven-thirty. They last about two hours."

"That's late!"

"It's tiring work, make no mistake. When the last act finishes, if we're moving on, Brown will tell us what time we need to set off. Depends on how far we've got to travel and the weather, but it's always early – five or six. You'll see more sunrises than you've seen before, I'll tell you that!"

"Five AM?!"

Larkin bit his fingernails before spitting them into the grass. "How can you be circus-folk and know nothing?"

"I'm not 'circus-folk'! I'd never even seen Pablo before yesterday."

"He says you stayed with him a few times when you was a baby."

I said grumpily, "I don't remember."

Larkin did the splits and then went over into a back bend. "Don't get so cross. You'll learn our ways quick enough."

I wasn't sure I would – this wasn't my world. I didn't

belong and Larkin would make sure I was constantly reminded of the fact, despite any surface similarities we might share. Why couldn't the Bellini brothers take me under their patronage instead?

"Ted. You learnt to walk, didn't you? And you can read? It's like that – none of us were born doing tricks or stunts."

"But you don't understand! I can't bend or jump or twist like you, and ... well ... Pablo will send me home when he finds out how useless I am. He won't want me here any longer." I crossed my arms sulkily. "And that's just fine."

"Ha!" Larkin crowed. "You got another think comin' if you reckon that's your way out!"

Polly poked her head out of the smaller tent and called over. "Come and get your tea while it's hot!"

"Come on, Teddy boy – I take it your legs work all right?"

Larkin and I raced over to the tent, almost elbowing each other on the way.

7.

After our tea, Larkin said we should head to the stables.

"But I've seen the horses already," I whined, as we made our way through the big tent, behind the curtains, to the makeshift stables. I didn't want to spend any more time with the horses than I needed to.

Larkin asked, "You ever had a horse?"

"No."

He rolled his eyes. "Well then, I best explain everything. Six o'clock, or earlier, the stables get cleaned out and the horses fed."

I should show *some* interest; maybe I could become a stablehand. "How often do you feed them?"

Larkin scattered oats from a sack into a long, low tray set out in front of the horses.

"With hay about three times a day, according to how hard they've worked. We graze them if they're not working. Pablo pays Brown extra to remove the dung, sweep out the stables and replace the straw. Those jobs need to be done every day."

"But if Brown does this, why tell me?"

"Everyone needs to know how to look after the horses. Don't you understand yet? A circus works together, as a *team*. Horses are like big dogs, each with their own personality. Look after them and they'll look after you. Know how to groom?"

I shook my head.

"You take a currycomb and curry him all over the body. Start at the neck."

Take a *what* and do *what*? "You may as well be speaking a different language!"

"Look!" He held up a comb that had a wooden handle and metallic teeth. "*This* is the currycomb."

He demonstrated on a chestnut horse. He moved swiftly and the horse remained calm under his expertise.

After I'd watched for a while, he said, "Here. Now you try."

I took the currycomb off him and slowly approached one of the brown ponies in the next stall. I was more at ease because they were smaller, and not as powerful-looking as the bigger breeds.

"Let him sniff you and then pet his head," Larkin called from the stall he was in. "They don't like being crept up on."

I faced the pony, but was trembling inside. "What if he bites?" I coughed, manure burning my nostrils.

"What are his ears doing?" Larkin sounded as if he couldn't believe he had been tasked with talking to someone so ignorant.

His attitude irritated me. "What have his ears got to do with anything?"

"His ears – are they sticking up, pointed at you?"

I nodded.

"You're fine then. If his ears are pinned flat against his head, don't approach. Let him sniff first."

I held out my hand, my stomach a tight ball. The pony sniffed at my palm lightly, his nostrils wet. I relaxed a little and petted his neck gently.

"You needn't be so gentle! He's no lady. A light touch will tickle. A firm pat is best."

My hand, stroking its neck, had only just stopped shaking. This was plenty for one day.

"Now that I've told you some of the basics, we can begin your *training*. Follow me, we'll go into the main ring where there's space."

"How about . . . starting off simple?" Larkin said, sitting on a bench in front of me. "Take your boots off. Can you touch your toes?"

I unlaced my boots and slipped them off. Then I

bent over, straining my fingertips towards my toes. Nope. Not a chance. My hands reached to my shins, at best, and there was a terrible tight pulling feeling in the back of my thighs.

"Is that it?" Larkin asked, his tone incredulous. "Is that as far as you can go?"

"Even this isn't ... comfortable," I wheezed from my bent-over position.

"It's not supposed to be COMFORTABLE!" Larkin roared. "You're going to have to practise *every day* or you'll never be flexible enough to turn tricks on a horse."

I snapped back, "Sleeping on a bench hasn't helped!"

He sighed. "Look, just ... start trying to pick up things with your toes. Try coins and stones and whatnot, and practise opening and closing your toes. You should wear your boots less too."

"When do the lions and elephants arrive?"

"Less talking and more stretching!" Larkin groaned. "We ain't got any of that. Sanger's had a lion that killed someone; Pablo doesn't want any more deaths on his hands. I've seen lions do tricks at other circuses, and they're glorious, but I've never seen them ... look happy."

I was finding it hard to breathe bent over like this. "You could say that about horses!"

"Look, copy me." Larkin stood up and started

lunging up and down. I tried my best to keep up.

"No. Wild beasts ain't the same as horses. Wait till you get used to them – they're so clever and they *like* us, if we're good to them. Anyway, a tiger cost more'n a week's profit and a lion double that! Business ain't the best. Pablo's not said much to me, not direct, but I've heard him complain to Brown. You hear a lot if you keep your ears open."

"What's the matter?"

"There's been fights about money." He lowered his voice. "Some people have left. I don't think Pablo can afford to hire in the acts he needs. And in the papers, there's people claiming circuses are bad. Polly said they're saying it's improper for ladies to be riding horses." He put his hand over his mouth and winked. "Especially with them hardly wearing any clothes!"

Then he changed, quick as storm clouds. His dark eyes flashed, and his mirth vanished. He pressed his lips together. "We need to prove them all wrong. They *have* to come and see that Pablo's is still the best."

"Is business so very bad?" Had I been brought here to help turn his fortune around? How was I to do that, knowing no tricks, having no skills?

"Other circuses are bigger. People will only go and see one 'cos that's all they can afford. The days of Pablo putting on free performances is over. We needs to show them something they ain't seen before. I'm working on a new turn, but Pablo's not had time to see it yet. We need novel ways to bring the crowds in!"

He sounded desperate, but this *was* his life and his home. And now it was mine too. I had a father. What did that even mean? Was Pablo only going to teach me how to ride, or were there other things he'd teach me too? And if his business was in trouble, would I be held to account if I couldn't come up with the goods? Or maybe he'd realize I wasn't worth the trouble and just send me home.

Larkin narrowed his eyes. "Are you tryin' to get out of training? Come on, back to it. Sit on the ground, put your feet flat together and make your legs into a diamond. Try to reach the ground with your knees."

As I grunted and strained, Larkin could barely keep his laughter in.

Eventually, I couldn't do it any longer. My thighs burned with effort and my toes were frozen. "I can't do this!" I wailed.

"You sound like a bairn."

"I don't care." My cheeks flamed. I wanted to be far away from this horrible stinking place.

"You won't get far with that attitude, I can tell you."

"You're not to tell me anything!" I sat on the bench, pulled on my boots and laced them angrily. I had a fierce temper. Sometimes, when George and I fought, as all brothers do, I said things in anger that I regretted. Mother often said I needed to think before I thought, let alone spoke.

I realized there was nowhere to go, but I needed to get away to clear my head.

"Where d'you think you're going?" Larkin asked, as I headed out of the tent. "We've barely started!"

"I need some air."

"There's plenty in here!"

"I want a rest. I'm *tired*. My legs hurt."

"They'll be hurting a good deal more than that soon. We haven't even gotten you on a horse yet! You can't just run off when things get burdensome. If you think that way, you'll spend half your life running!"

I didn't care to listen to any more of Larkin's wisdom. I dashed out into the fresh air, leaving his stupid words inside the big tent with him.

8.

Polly was washing out some bowls. Feeling sorry for myself, I went over to her, hoping for a smile or a kind word, perhaps.

"Hallo," she smiled briefly, but went back to cleaning her crockery.

I kicked at the ground, annoyed with myself, now that I was standing in front of her with an empty mind. "Anything I can help with?" I asked.

"Actually, there is. See that wagon?" She pointed about fifteen feet away. "It's packed up, but up on the top is a bag of material samples that I need. If you could reach them for me, that'd be very kind."

I sprinted to the wagon and hopped on to the back of it, which was narrow, almost like a beam. I walked along, balanced carefully, so I could stretch up to reach the top of the pile. I thought of George and me running along the walls at home. What were Mother and George doing at this moment? Had they set off to find his medicine? Did they miss me as much as I missed them?

I ran back and handed the bag to Polly.

"You was fast! Thank you. What else can you do, apart from climb like a cat?" Her eyes twinkled. "Can you sew?"

I shook my head.

"Well, then, I can't think of much else that needs doing." She placed a cup on the wagon step and glanced around with her hands on her hips. "The horses have been fed. We got a performance this afternoon, another this evening and then that's it, we'll be packing up, pulling down to move on."

"Pulling what?"

"What do you think, silly! Pulling the *tent* down. You'll be needed then, I'm sure. It's all hands on deck. Hard work that is."

Larkin caught up to me. He took my arm and dragged me across the field. "Look here," he said, chewing a length of straw. "Don't be so sore! You got to put more effort in, that's all. You won't be no expert right off."

I shook him off, angrily. "I don't care about being an 'expert'! I didn't want to come here in the first place."

He frowned. "Well, that's as maybe, but you're here

now. We don't get much choice about what *we* want, right? As long as you've got food and a place to sleep, then I reckon you're doing all right in this life. Trust me. I been worse places, seen worse things."

"So have I," I replied, thinking of the steel mills and their brutal heat, the smell and sharp particles of hot steel that George and I would sometimes get pierced with, and later try to pick out with a pin. Staying at work till eight at night and sometimes even ten, with only half an hour for breakfast and an hour for dinner. Sometimes we'd fall asleep at our work, stumbling when the metal flooring got hot and slippery.

"It's no good grumbling, Ted. You might dream about being elsewhere, but sometimes you got to open your eyes and face what's in front of you. If you don't like what you see, only *you* can change that. I mean, maybe not *where* you are, but how you think about it. Your attitude."

Larkin was speaking to me as if I was a halfwit. How dare he!

"I know that! I'm not stupid."

"I never said you were, but I ain't seen half a smile cross your face today, neither. My folks are dead. I lived on the streets. You don't seem to know a good thing when it's right in front of you! Circus life is a *good* life, especially in the spring and summertime. And on Sundays, Pablo sends us off to church. Insists on it."

"Sermons aren't fun."

"No, dummy. We never actually *go* to church. We have a lark. You gotta make the best of whatever you've got, see? If you *can't* do that, then you're stupider than I thought it possible for any boy to be."

"What do *you* know?" Before I'd even thought of the words, they hurtled out of my thoughtless mouth. "*You're* just a common chimney sweep."

Silence.

"That's as maybe," he said, quietly. "But at least I got manners, which is more 'n I can say for you. The circus is a place for the unusual and the heroic. You don't seem to be either of them things," Larkin sneered.

"Never said I was," I said, sulkily.

"Stop getting ... so worked up. Look. *Everyone* wants to be special. Everyone wants to be able to do something that other people can't. But if you're not special, then the next best thing is to be close to someone, or something, that *is*. We give the crowds who pay to see us time to be special. Don't you want to be a part of something special?"

"I'm already a part of something – my *family*, thank you very much!"

He creased his brow. "I don't see what you're thanking me for. . ."

"I'm *not*!" This boy was as dense as he was flexible!

My blood was still bubbling, although it wasn't quite as hot as before. Most of my fire had snuffed out. Larkin knew how life was around here and I didn't. Besides, what choice did I have? *None.* I tried to quiet the scorching roar inside me and imagined Mother's hand against my cheek, and heard her kind voice, patiently urging me to calm down.

I stared at the ground, biting my lip. Maybe I needed to be candid if I wanted Larkin as a friend. If I wanted any friends at all.

"And what if. . ." My voice was shrinking. "What if. . . I'm no good? At any of it? I don't want to ride horses. I don't even like them!"

"You don't have to like them, but if you ain't going to ride, if you ain't even willing to try . . . then you'll be stuck clearing out their muck. That's the grimmest job there is. All you got to do with horses is show 'em who's boss."

"Says you."

"Yep. Says *me*," Larkin bragged, sticking his fingers in his pockets and grinning.

He appeared to be utterly happy with his life here. Nothing seemed to bother him for long.

There was no escaping that this was my new life, and, no matter how uncertain I was, or how I longed for the sweet comfort of home (even the hot sparks from the steel mill didn't seem so terrible), this life *did* come with Larkin for company. Although he was no substitute for George, life would be even lonelier if I had no friends. He was correct – I had food to fill my stomach. And tonight, I'd make sure I was settled in the sleeping tent, snuggled up amongst the straw.

9.

I hadn't even watched a performance yet. I'd kept myself busy all afternoon, helping prepare stew instead. I knew that all eyes would be on me once I entered that big tent. I knew I couldn't avoid it forever. Pablo would expect me to be full of excitement and enthusiasm for the evening show, but the minute I heard the bell signalling the start of the performance, all I felt was terror.

I entered the tent nervously and could only watch for a few minutes before I ducked out, my heart thudding so loud I imagined everyone could hear it, even over all the noise.

After the pulldown afterwards, which I hadn't realized would take so long – or that canvas could weigh so much – we travelled long hours along the uneven roads. Brown, Larkin, Polly and I travelled in one wagon, the Bellini brothers and Clara in the other, while Pablo went on ahead, riding Bessie, who pulled his living wagon. Other wagons, with the stronger horses pulling them, were in-between us. The horses were tired, all of us exhausted, dozing on the way.

Part of me longed to appreciate the hedgerows and scenery, but all I could think about was how quickly our presence had been cleared away – how only a flattened patch of ground had revealed that there had been any life at all!

Where were we going? I heard names of places I didn't know. Where was Hebden Bridge? How long would this circus tour last, and how far would it take me from my home?

I spotted a sparrow and wished that Mother or George were with me, so I could share the experience. As the wagon wheels rattled, I wondered: when would I see them again? Had George gotten his medicine? Was I expected to become so accomplished that I'd be able to help by sending money home?

The roads were lumpy and bumpy. Several times the wagon wheels caught in ditches and we needed to put boards under the wheels and heave each other out. Thankfully, the wheels on Pablo's living wagon were so high that they didn't get stuck in the potholes or water-logged streets.

I might have grumbled some . . . I was tired.

"Stop complaining! You ought to try doing this in the rain!" Larkin jeered at one point, after I'd slipped over twice in the mud. He'd spent much of the ride cracking jokes at my expense, trying to impress Polly, so I'd stopped speaking to him, wondering about his value as a friend after all.

Instead, to keep myself awake, I asked Brown about the circus life, and how things worked.

Brown said, "Our troupe used to be much bigger. We had thirty horses with clowns, a ring master and a big band at one time. Mr Arnold put up wooden amphitheatres – those temporary buildings you asked about before – and we'd perform there during winter. When we rolled into Bolton, twenty years ago, Pablo rode through those streets – such horsemanship to control twelve horses! That stunt brought us considerable publicity. He works tirelessly. I reckon circus folk are the hardest working but most cheerful people I've ever known. Yet, I can see, quite plain, that you've no interest in being here."

I rushed to tell him he was mistaken, but he held up his hand. "No need to explain, lad. I'm surprised, but there you are. Circus life ain't for everyone. But Pablo's circus is still going. If you learn nothing else in your time spent with us – if you *listen* to nothing else – you listen to the fact that he is *still* going. What does that say about a person? That twenty-five years later, he's still here, trying? The circus became his home, his *family*, and you never give up on what, or who, you love. And, even if he weren't there for you before, you mark my words, my boy, he'll certainly be there for you now. You'd do best to remember that."

He fell into silence. As we passed quiet and empty streets, I thought of all the people inside their homes, sleeping soundly. And here we were bumping up and down on uneven roads with wagons filled to the brim. These sleeping folk had no idea that the circus was about to descend upon them in only a few hours.

I asked, "How do people know to come and see us?" Were we welcome? Did folk like having the circus around?

Larkin tutted, loudly. "Everyone knows when we're coming!"

I ignored him, and turned pointedly towards Brown, who said, "We used to have a manager and it was his job to arrive at each place a few days before us, to tell people we were coming."

"Do they like having their town taken over?" I asked.

"Course they do!" Larkin answered. "A few days of colour, noise and excitement! Who wouldn't like it? Round these parts, people might not be able to travel to see a bigger circus. I reckon for some folks it's the highlight of their year!"

Being a manager sounded like a safe, non-dangerous job, maybe even something I could offer to help with. "What else does a manager do?"

"Hires the grounds. Puts announcements in the newspapers and finds acts. But now, well, I do most of that. We all help put up posters on walls and bridges – anywhere in town where people might see. We still have tent men though; they go on with the baggage-wagons to put the tent up. When we get there, we make up the ring, fix the hurdles and gates and make sure the horses are stabled, groomed and fed."

Despite myself, my tummy started tingling. Getting the circus ready in a new place, with no riding needed, at least not yet, sounded exciting.

"What else?"

"You'll see soon enough!" His eyes shone.

The wagons clattered into an open field. This field wasn't as far from civilisation as the one we'd just left. Across the way was an orchard and huge oaks lined the edges.

"Let us unload then." Pablo climbed down from Bessie. Today he wore a drab overcoat, with a broad collar and cuffs of lambskin. He snapped his cuffs.

"We've till noon to get ready." He nodded to Brown and the Bellini brothers. "Then we'll stable the horses and make sure they're fed and groomed."

Fog settled thick atop the field. It was early and a little dusky. From across the field, I watched as a group of men put up the big tent. No wonder they stayed in a building during wintertime! This would be harsh in the cold and snow.

Larkin hopped off the wagon, helped Polly down and then said to me, "That's the tent master."

We watched him drive an iron spike, about eight inches long, into the hard ground. From the top of the spike flapped a band of string and round it the men traced a circle into the ground with sticks, perhaps thirty or forty feet in diameter. Then they unloaded poles and heavy rolls of canvas off the wagons and spread everything out on the ground. With four great masts, poles and ropes, the tent was heaved into place. The men worked as a team, their movements almost seamless. There was laughing and joking and singing too, to start with, but after a while, grunts and curses about chaffed hands and muddy boots echoed in the morning air, making me very glad that I hadn't been asked to help.

Polly, Clara and the Bellini brothers rummaged in wagons and filled buckets with water. I followed them into the now-erected big tent.

Brown turned to me, smiling. "Now we help build the ring itself."

Everyone threw buckets of water into the middle. Larkin grinned. "I enjoy this bit! Just copy what I do."

We levelled the ground by stamping down as hard as we could. Now the earth was wet and mixed with sawdust, it all stuck together. I didn't mind doing this and was glad to see that the circus wasn't only performing terrifying stunts.

Pablo and Brown bolted together the sections of wood that formed the ring enclosure, marked it with ropes, acting like barriers, and then that was it – the big tent was up and ready!

Despite myself, pride fluttered in my chest and I couldn't stop smiling.

"Good job!" Pablo bellowed. "Ted? Come! I wish to show you something."

I followed him to where the stables had been made up. The horses were settled and Pablo was petting a dark brown horse.

"This is Napoleon. He's one of our biggest, about seventeen hands. Larkin says you've not ridden yet? Here, feed him from your hand."

There was no avoiding it now. I took the carrot Pablo offered me and laid it flat on my palm, praying

Napoleon wouldn't bite my hand. Hairy lips tickled my palm as he took it. I had my eyes half-squeezed shut.

"He's looking upon you as a friend already. That's how they learn to obey you."

I watched, fascinated, as Pablo gave the horse little taps on one of his forelegs. Napoleon went down easily on one knee and then the other knee followed.

"Once in this position, the horse will submit to being gently rolled over on to his side, as though in a trance. Let each act be gentle, and he will be content. They have good memories do horses, and they're clever too. You're not dealing with dumb animals here, m'boy. One of Astley's horses used to make tea!"

"Make tea?" I laughed. "Whatever do you mean?"

"He could lift a kettle off a fire! Now, are you ready to ride?"

"Oh no, not yet." I shook my head. "I hurt my back yesterday, trying to tumble." I tried to sound enthusiastic. "Maybe tomorrow?"

Pablo searched my face keenly. I don't think he believed me because his own face lost its smile and his eyes dulled. "Let us sit you on one anyway. See how it feels. Come on, son. Often the idea of a thing is worse than the thing itself."

Pablo led Napoleon out into the ring. I followed slowly behind, dragging my feet as much as I could. How could I avoid this now? I couldn't. I gulped and clenched my hands into fists at my side.

This was it. I was going to have to climb on a horse and face my worst fear.

10.

"Brown says you've been all over. Have you been on a ship?" I asked, hoping talk might prove a distraction. "America, perhaps?"

"Oh no, Ted. A man of my ... colour, over there, would never become as successful as I've become here. They've only just stopped using us as slaves. And now ... well, now I'm too old to think of travelling so far."

"What do you mean?"

"Slavery might well be illegal in Britain, with the abolition act, but America has a different attitude. They aren't quite there yet, it seems to me." He nodded slowly, his expression serious and a little sad. "One person should never own another."

"But, isn't that just the same as an apprenticeship?" I asked, interested, but mainly trying to keep Pablo talking, hoping he'd forget about getting me up on Napoleon.

"Not the same at all! Apprenticeships teach new skills and provide a future, sometimes for those who might not have one otherwise. Slavery? That's quite different. Who decides that one man is better than another? No, it is not correct. Enough with your chatter – let's get you on this horse!"

Napoleon stood still as Pablo dragged over a mounting block and set it next to him. "Now we have some space so that he doesn't feel cramped, you see."

I wished the tent would collapse, trapping us all under it. Anything, anything not to have to climb up on this horse. My breathing was fast and I started to feel dizzy.

"This block will help. I'll hold him. Make sure he's paying you attention and not trying to walk off. Always mount from the horse's left-hand side."

I climbed up the mounting block, my palms sweaty and thudding heartbeat loud. Pablo's instructions sounded as if they came from very far away.

"Put the reins over his head so they'll be in the correct position when you mount. Left foot in the stirrup, shift your weight over and swing your other leg over the top of the horse. Go on, boy, on you get!"

I did a little jump and tried to throw my leg over.

"No!" Pablo yelled. "Don't grab on to the back of the saddle or else it'll slip!"

Finally, I hauled my leg over. I felt so high off the ground – too high. Napoleon started swaying his head, and my stomach churned. "You're on. Good. Now, before you sit down, put both feet in the stirrups." Pablo made adjustments to them, so they'd fit.

Were Napoleon's ears pinned back? How could I tell from this position? Why had Pablo put me on such a big horse?

"Have you those reins tightly?"

I could barely sit astride this animal, let alone ride it! Did Pablo expect me to eventually be able to stand up and balance? I suddenly felt faint; my hands slackened on the reins. Napoleon twitched and as I leaned away from his head, my foot came out of the stirrup and I wobbled.

"How do I get down?" I asked quietly, trembling, my eyes filling with tears.

"Take both feet out of the stirrups and then swing off. If you keep your foot in the stirrup and the horse spooks, then you might get dragged."

Pablo held Napoleon firm while I climbed off, shaking from head to toe.

His tone was light, but he must have been frustrated and disappointed with me. "Not riding today then. P'raps tomorrow." Pablo patted the horse's neck firmly. He stroked his moustache, gazing upwards. "Yes. You'll be ready to ride then. We'll begin with trotting and cantering. Now, fetch Larkin, and you help the ladies with whatever they need."

He *was* disappointed. He thought me only fit enough to be off with the women. He wanted Larkin. Of course he did. Larkin was more his son than I'd ever be.

I wandered slowly out of the tent into the field, wiping at my eyes, which kept filling with tears as I realized what a failure I must be to Pablo.

The sky had darkened, and rain was on its way. I trudged past the sleeping and costume tents and down to the end of the field we'd settled in, by the trees at the bottom.

I rubbed my eyes, not sure what I was seeing. Larkin was sneaking a bag off one of the wagons. By the way he checked around and then dashed behind a tree, he was clearly doing something he shouldn't have been. Most of the troupe were busy fixing gas lamps around the tent and I don't think anyone else had noticed him.

I rounded the thick tree trunk to see him leaning against the other side, stuffing bread and cheese into his mouth with the speed of a locomotive.

"What are you doing?"

He jumped about three feet and with his other hand, pushed something down deep in his pocket.

"What are *you* doing here? You should be practising stretching and bending, like yesterday. Unless ..." His eyes glittered. "Don't think by doing nothing that Pablo will give up on you. That ain't gonna happen."

I couldn't take his nonsense any longer. "Who made you Lord and Master?"

"We've a tour booked. If Pablo wants you in the show, then you'll be in the show. That's all I'll say."

"All you'll say? Pah! You've said a fine lot and more besides! What are *you* doing here more like."

Swallowing his mouthful, he struggled to speak. "I'm hungry!"

"What's in there?" I asked, pointing to his bulging pockets.

He grimaced and pulled out three fat sausages, shamefaced. They smelled glorious and my mouth fair watered at the sight of them. They'd been cooked last night and were supposed to be our lunch.

"Want one?" he asked, sullenly.

Yes! my stomach growled. *That's* why he'd sneaked down to this secluded end of the field.

He smirked, holding one out and waving it. "Go on, mate."

I didn't want to be associated with his thievery. "Not likely!" I shouted.

He sniffed. "Don't say nothin'. Please," he wheedled.

"Why not? You're a fraud – talking about teamwork but then stealing!"

"You're impossible to help."

"How do you figure that?"

Larkin grumbled, "You complain all the time. Looking down your nose at us." Staring at me defiantly, he crammed a whole sausage into his mouth. "Likes of you have had it easy, at home with Mother, never getting your hands dirty."

"I have *not*! Me and George worked."

Larkin spat, just missing my boots. "Haven't we all?"

He was only a year older than me but presumed he knew everything! My blood sizzled again. I gritted my teeth and glared at him.

"Ever been in a steel mill? Up close to those blistering sparks?"

He stepped so close that our noses were almost touching. "You? A mill? Ever been up a ruddy chimney? Them places are so cramped that every day I crawled up one, I thought my chest would cave in. They're dark, they stink, and it's boiling more than a pig on a spit; you don't think you'll ever make it out. Every day could be your last. Know what *that's* like? Living like that – all the time believing death is coming?"

We glared at each other, eyes like red-hot fire irons.

Were we really competing for whose life had been harshest?

Larkin broke off eye contact first. He muttered wearily, "Ted. If you've slept in a bed, no matter how small or hard, and no matter how hungry you've been, *none* of that compares with what I been through."

He rubbed his hands over his face. "You don't know what I've had to do. I been in jail." His voice cracked.

"Jail?" I rested my hand on the tree trunk, the cool firm bark comforting. "That doesn't surprise me with your light fingers!"

Larkin bowed his head and gazed at the ground for such a long time that the fire in my stomach died away, leaving only embers.

"It was no joke, Ted. I was in jail for two months. Felt like half my life. I had to work in silence all day, till I practically dropped down dead. I'd only taken a scrap of coal to keep my little brother warm." His confidence was stripped away now; he sounded fearful and miserable, and as if he'd forgotten I was even there.

Jail?

He started shaking his head and didn't stop, still disbelieving. "We got flogged; I got scars all over. I was hungry for so long that I stopped being hungry and . . . felt like I was floating instead, like I was already dead. That'll happen when people stop treating you like a person. When they kick and punch and call you names. Couldn't sleep. Needed to stay alert 'cos sometimes the older ones started beatin' on me, for no reason, like it was a sport.

"Up and down chimneys weren't much better, but then, least I was too busy just tryin' to stay alive ... so my head had no room for wondering if life might be any different.

"But being locked up? Your mind gets to thinking, and that's not the best thing for a mind, is it? 'Cos once you start, you can't stop. What if Ma and Pa and Bobby hadn't got the cholera? We never had much, but we always had each other."

I didn't know what to say. I'd been unfair in my judgement of Larkin, without knowing the facts. No wonder he never stayed downcast for long. He and Pablo had that in common; I could see now that was how they survived. By bouncing back and never giving in. They lived like that because for them, there was no other way. Seeing the best in things, their unfailing optimism wasn't a quality to be scorned, it was ... admirable, and absolutely necessary for their survival.

"Larkin, I'm sorry. That sounds ... horrible. *Terrible*. But if you're hungry, just ask Pablo for more; I'm sure he'd give it. Stealing is no way to behave."

"But I already had my share. What if Pablo can

only afford to feed one growing lad? What if . . ." He turned away slightly, started scuffing his boot along the ground. "What if there ain't enough food to go around? What if he had to choose between me and you, eh? I don't want to put that idea in his head 'cos who d'ya think he'd choose?"

I sighed. "You, probably."

"Not bleedin' likely. You're his *son*. His flesh and blood. Listen. I promised him I'd make you the best young rider – next to me – but 'cos of your pig-headedness, he reckons me a liar! He's cross you ain't made progress yet. I can't have it. I been *trying* to help you. Even though—"

"Even though what?" I snapped.

"Even though . . . helping you might be the end for me! Don't you understand?"

"What?"

"You might end up *better* than me. Riding is in your blood, isn't it? Riding horses is what you were 'born to do', so Pablo keeps telling everyone."

"As far as I can tell, I'm not born to do anything. Well, nothing related to the circus," I said.

Larkin scoffed, "Don't let Pablo hear you say that. *He* believes the circus – family – is everything, with every bone in his body. Never seen him so happy as he is now with you knocking about the place." He shrugged, rubbing his head and frowning. "Maybe it's time I moved on, anyway. I can't see he'll have much use for us both, not once you can ride. He's hardly looked my way since you came; I showed him new flips, tried to tell him about ideas for a new act, but he wasn't even interested."

"Come on..." I patted his arm. "No need for thinking that. I won't say a word about it, but please . . . don't steal food again. We all have to eat."

"You're not so bad at giving out lectures yourself." He sounded brighter.

"If we try to get along, there *will* be room for us both. I'm not your rival. Pablo wants me to ride, but I'm useless. I'll never be any good with the horses. But perhaps you could help me find something I *am* good at instead?"

"I seen you run. You're fast. Can you balance? What about the rope?"

I shook my head. "No, I don't want to do that. Not after seeing that woman fall. There must be other things. And you're right, I should try to do what Pablo wants. I'll try, if you'll teach me."

"Lemme look through that picture tube in that sack of yours every now and then and you got yourself a deal. We'll find something that ain't the horses."

11.

I'd been with Pablo's troupe for almost three weeks now and I'd done little more than a trot around the ring, white-knuckled, my heart in my throat the entire time.

I was feeding the horses, not as frightened of them as I once was, finding their presence peaceful in a way . . . when Pablo marched over.

"Getting to know the horses, are you?" he smiled, pleased.

I fussed with a bridle. "I like the ponies." And I did, though it didn't mean I wanted to ride them. I carefully washed the bit that went into Nightingale's mouth, and dried it.

Pablo winked. "They remind me of women; sweet-natured, *if* things are going their way!"

I wasn't expecting him to find me here. I'd heard him and the tent master having a heated discussion about wages and thought he had important circus matters to attend to.

I'd been wondering about Pablo's life. Mostly while laying on my lumpy mattress night after night, trying to drown out Brown's snoring and Larkin's night-time mutterings while I flipped through *Varney the Vampire*.

"Sir, when you were my age, what was your favourite circus thing?"

"Horse stunts and then rope walking. The rope tells us much about life."

"How so?"

"Rope walking lets you determine whether you play it safe, or take a risk. You determine everything. On a horse, there is speed, certainly, and you must consider the animal, as well as yourself and how you affect one another. But up on the rope, it is only *you* and the rope. It's focused and ... pure."

"It's dangerous," I said, polishing a harness with wax paste. "I saw a woman die at Aston Park."

I had no idea if Mother had told him about the event or not.

"I know," he replied quietly. "It must have been an awful shock, Ted."

"It was."

"But, it wasn't her who slipped, it was the rope that

broke. Snapped right in two. Only a monster would have put a woman who was with child up on that rope. I knew Selina well. We knew each other for many years. She was very talented. She should have stopped performing, but she had her husband Edward, seven children and her mother to support. A tragedy that easily could have been avoided."

"I don't think I'm cut out for the circus, sir," I almost held my breath saying these words. "Could I be ... could I be a stable boy instead, perhaps? Or, how about your next manager, going on ahead?"

He roared with laughter. I had no idea why – what was so amusing? – but his laugh was infectious, and I couldn't help but smile.

"Ted! *I* was born in a workhouse. How is that being 'cut out' for the circus? We managed to leave the workhouse after a few years, but life inside was hard. Must have been over six hundred of us cramped up in that dark place, spinning wool and twisting it into threads all day. Where is your spirit of adventure? There's no limit to what you can achieve if you're prepared to work. I made *my* way."

"But you did that because you had to!" I said, peevishly.

"I viewed every opportunity that came my way as an adventure, that's how I managed. I never said 'No', or 'I can't', until I'd tried! And I was always smiling and polite. I made extra effort, Ted. Even if everyone I met believed a workhouse orphan might never amount to much, I showed them that's not true. You can do the same!"

I wasn't convinced. From what I'd observed, it struck me that one needed a certain temperament to be a proper circus person; a person who could stand up and talk in this way. Larkin had the same attitude. I doubted it could be taught.

This ... *circus spirit* was either in you or it wasn't. I saw nothing of myself reflected in this bold, confident man.

Pablo put his hand on my shoulder and squeezed gently. "I wanted you ... I *hoped* you'd have a better start in life than I had, Ted. That was why, when your mother wished to settle down and move away, I didn't mind. I'd already lost one woman I loved. I did not wish to lose another. But I always wanted to have my boys back with me one day."

"I'm sorry about your wife."

"It was a dreadful night. I rushed to move the heavy timbers that had fallen on her. I carried her in my arms to the nearest tavern. I ran! A surgeon was called for, but there was nothing that could be done."

I didn't know this before. Larkin and Brown's

accounts of the accident had never said how he tried to save her.

He coughed. "Come, we need to get ready." Pablo slid the bit into Bessie's mouth and held the bridle up over her nose.

"What for?"

"Advertising, my boy! Who will know where or who we are unless we tell them? We need to thrust handbills into people's hands. Make them curious. That's how we draw in the crowds. Sheldon used to advertise our arrival; he was a genius. But it falls to us these days."

I didn't think before I asked, "Can you not afford Sheldon now?"

He busied himself fixing up Bessie ready to ride. I had spoken out of turn.

"Well," he said eventually, "Sheldon moved on. But the more we do ourselves, the more we work as a team, then there is less to pay others and . . . the more there will be for us. Advertising is essential. You, Larkin and Polly take a wagon into town. Polly can buy supplies, and you and Larkin can stick billposters about."

*

The weather was clement for a ride. The three of us rode for just less than an hour, travelling about ten miles, to Bolton, near the abbey, which was where we'd

97

be performing next.

Larkin secured the horse and wagon outside The Craven Arms and helped Polly down, smirking. He'd hardly said two words to me the whole journey, though he'd kept his tongue wagging at her. Every time Polly was near, he acted as if I didn't exist.

"Where shall we start then, Larkin?"

"We?" He slipped an arm around Polly's waist, and laughed when she playfully slapped his arm away. "You don't expect me to leave this lovely lady on her lonesome, do you? You can take care of the leaflets. Meet us here in a couple of hours. We'll hand out some across town."

But Pablo had said for us to do it together! *Fine.* I thought Larkin had changed his tune after our recent discussion, but if he didn't want to come along with me then I didn't want him around.

I'd give out so many handbills, and shout about the circus so loud, that Pablo would have only me to thank when the crowds were so thick that there wasn't enough seating!

Larkin and Polly headed up the road away from me, so I turned on my heel.

From the village green I went through a gap in the wall. "Afternoon! Lovely day!"

A couple out walking looked at me, frowning a

little. I'd seen similar frowns before. Probably because of the colour of my skin. Well, what did that matter now? I had a job to do, and no amount of frowning was going to stop me!

They didn't even glance at the handbills I waved in front of them. No wonder Pablo wanted Larkin and I to do this together! Larkin probably would have turned a tumble or two to impress them.

I'd need to try harder, that was all. I could do this. I needed to show Pablo something I was good at.

"Hello! How are you? Here, please would you like a bill about the circus? We're coming to the green soon." I smiled, pressing handbills into the palms of passers-by.

I'd handed out a few and had been glad to notice old playbills stuck up on hoardings. I stopped to read the full advert.

People clearly liked the circus; their faces lit up when they read their handbills. "Ooh, the African Prince!" a couple said, nodding at each other.

That was Pablo! Inside, I beamed.

Some people just hurried on by, of course. I steered clear of the busier roads, smiled at a flower girl and wished I had pennies for a pie. My belly grumbled. I had no idea of the time. I must have been walking for at least an hour. The road thinned out to quiet lanes and the sound of my boots echoed.

There were large hollows, dips, on either side of a meadow. I followed the path past the priory towards the river. I figured I'd stumbled across a shortcut, but I shouldn't have come this way; there were fewer people around.

I heard animal noises behind me. "Ooo-ooo!"

I recognized the sound: the noise a monkey might make. And there was no mistaking it – this was no friendly 'coo-eee'. This wasn't young children having fun; these noises were guttural and threatening.

The hairs on the back of my neck stood up. I quickened my pace. The noises coming from behind me grew louder.

12.

I clenched my handbills and walked faster. I didn't turn around because if I stopped to acknowledge them, things might get worse.

I knew it was a group of boys because of their snorting laughter. How many might there be?

"Oi! Show us yer tricks, circus boy!" a boy hollered.

Another boy started making ape noises.

George and I had been called names in the street because of our skin colour, although not too often. Further trouble had been avoided because we'd just run straight home and got ourselves safe behind closed doors, where we didn't have to consider those horrible names, or how angry and sad they made us. But here, now, there was nowhere to run, and worse still, I was alone.

What would George do if he were here? What would Larkin do, or Pablo for that matter?

"You show-off circus folk think you're special."

"We want an advance show. See if it's worth paying pennies for later, which it probably ain't!" Gales of laughter followed.

"Oi!" A harder voice, full of thunderclouds, chimed in. "My father says the darker the skin the smaller the brain – that true?"

My bladder prickled; they sounded closer now. If I ran, they might give chase, and then there was no telling what they'd do if they caught me. How many were there? Should I turn and face them? I was going to be sick.

"We should bash his head open to find out!"

I halted. I'd stopped so suddenly I feared they would crash into the back of me, and although I was no rider or acrobat, I wasn't a coward either.

Furious, I turned round to see who dared speak such dark, horrifying words.

Five boys. *Five!* Bigger and older than me. Two of them had whiskers, and all wore tight little sneers.

I stood no chance!

Four of them took up a fighting stance, and the other boy, the stockiest, hunkered down and then charged with both arms out, shoving me in the middle of my chest.

I rocketed backwards but didn't fall over.

"Looks like he's been eating mud!"

"Ha! Push 'im harder! Go on. You can get him

down if you try hard enough."

They circled round and pushed me back and forth amongst them, like I was a ragdoll. Something wet and foul struck my cheek – spittle.

I couldn't escape now. I had no idea what to do. I closed my eyes and murmured a silent prayer.

THWACK!

A punch, especially one you don't see coming, is a mighty surprise.

CRACK!

My nose! I dropped to my knees. Instinct kicked in and I shielded my face with my arms, covering my head as best I could, but they were grabbed and pinned behind my back. My cheek was struck.

In my mind, I blocked my ears to the taunts. I prayed this would all be over soon. I squeezed my eyes tight, trying to conjure up Mother's voice and remember comforting words she'd say late at night, if George and I had had a bad day. 'You're my boys. *My* boys. You pay those wicked words no mind. The two of you are perfect. There is nothing wrong with you. Kindness is not a colour and nor is humility, or grace. You hush now and do not think any more about it!'

If I said and did nothing, perhaps they'd move on to some other awful sport. But it took them a while before they tired of terrorising me.

I was kicked in the ribs. My fingers were grabbed and stamped on. I tried to curl further and further into myself and then the world went black.

"You all right there?" A voice: young and sweet.

I tried opening my eyes, but it was a monumental effort. I licked my lips, only to find them puffy and sticky: blood. My head pounded like the mallets hammering the stakes into the circus ground.

She cleared her throat. "Can you sit up?"

I managed to open one eye to see a small, skinny girl kneeling over me. White-faced and freckled, with sticky-up black hair, and a white pinafore covered in so much mud you couldn't be sure it had ever been white. She wore four or five ragged coats layered on top of one another. One was missing buttons, and the one I glimpsed underneath had huge tears.

We were next to a riverbank. She gripped my elbow and helped me into a sitting position. "Them lads! What pigs!"

She spat into the mud. "I threw an old shoe I found at one's head and screamed 'Murder!' so loud they took off in a fright. Serves them right." She grinned, revealing a large gap between her top teeth and a chipped, jagged bottom row. "Wish I'd had a rock to bash them with. They fair beat you to mush."

"Th-thank you," I stuttered, not sure if I'd spoken aloud. My head hurt, my ribs ached and I urgently needed the privy.

"What are these?" She brandished scraps of the handbills I'd been giving out; they'd been torn to shreds. "Is this what they was after?"

"I-I'm with the circus. I was telling people about our next show and they just—" I couldn't bring myself to speak of any more. The thought that I could be so hated, hated enough to be beaten by strangers, simply on account of the colour of my skin, or for being from the circus, or both, made me sick to my stomach. Sick and sad and as helpless and hopeless as I'd ever known.

Wasn't life difficult enough? I remembered Mother's warm arms and squeezed my eyes closed against hot tears. I threw an arm across my face so that this girl wouldn't see.

"Hey, now!" she said, sounding firm and fierce. "You're all right now. Come on. Don't take on so! You ain't got nothin' broken; I don't think anyways. They weren't upon you but a second." She rubbed her grubby palm in the grass before holding it out, nails filthy and raggedy. "Alma."

I sniffed. "Ted."

"Can I call you Teddy?"

"No!"

"Circus, eh? That sounds magical. Is it?" Her eyes shone like little chips of amber.

I sighed. "I'm new. Not sure I've seen much magic so far," I griped. "Why are you out here? Where are your folks?"

She started picking mud and dried grass off her pinafore. "I runned away."

"From who?"

"Not who. *Where*. The workhouse, and I can't go back. Now I'm collecting stuff and selling it, if I'm lucky. I got me fingers in a few pies."

"What do you collect?"

"Stuff that I find down here by the river. There's all sorts of treasures thrown away that gets washed up. Coal, iron, copper. I get a good price for it."

"Oi! Ted!"

I turned to see Larkin running full pelt towards us. He arrived panting and swearing. "Been looking all over for you! Cripes. Look at the state of you! Whatever has happened?"

We explained. Larkin didn't interrupt, but his face grew serious and his eyes narrow and cold. "Those blockheads!" He uttered more profanities, which shocked me so much I almost put my hands over Alma's ears.

At last he said, "Polly's at the wagon. It'll be dark

soon. We'd better get going."

"Larkin, this is my friend, Alma."

"Hullo, Alma." Larkin looked her up and down properly now; he sniffed and wrinkled his nose. "Come *on* Ted, let us get moving."

"I'm comin' and all," Alma said, shoving handfuls of junk into her pockets and wiping her nose with her coat sleeve.

"Says who?" Larkin said.

"Says me. I saved your friend and I wanna see him in the circus."

Larkin rolled his eyes. Alma may have been tiny, but we both knew this was a Miss to be reckoned with.

"Fine," we both said together.

From behind, Larkin put his arms round my waist and hauled me to my feet in one swift, strong movement. He and Alma, on either side of me, dragged me limping, along the path, mud collecting up under my boots. I could barely see out of one eye; it was swelling shut. My upper lip was wet and warm, and every time my tongue touched it, I felt the slickness of blood. Trying to draw breath felt like my insides were creaking apart.

I must have been sniffling or crying because Larkin sounded gentle, and murmured, over and over, "Don't fret. We're nearly there, at the wagon. We'll clean you up. It will be all right. You just need to ... rest." His voice cracked a little as he whispered, "You're going to be all right."

The three of us dragged each other along, shambling but undefeated, and the abbey, magnificent and eternal, rose up in front of us out of the dusk, stretching right up into the sky.

13.

Upon entering the circus tent, Pablo boomed, "What has happened?" and Larkin, in low tones, explained. The words came as if from far away. I was dimly aware of Alma's hand on my arm and of water and cloths being requested. I was helped to sit down, but had no idea of much else.

Pablo's breathing sounded quick and angry as he fired questions. "Who?" and "Where?" and "Why?" and Larkin replied, "Ted says they called us slaves and savages. That we deserve nothing better than to live tied up and in cages."

Pablo strode over to where I was propped against a bench. He stared into my one open eye and tenderly touched his fingertips to it. "Let me help you clean up."

His voice was like a caress. He eased me sideways on to a pile of straw. He dipped a cloth into a bowl of water and squeezed it out, his voice subdued as he spoke.

"People are attracted to, and fearful of, that which they do not have occasion to witness every day. Do you understand, Ted?"

He stroked the cloth over my forehead and dabbed gently under my eye, which was almost swollen shut.

As he did this, I stopped thinking about Mother. All thoughts about her ceased as it occurred to me that Pablo was being as gentle as Mother would have been, if she were here. He was taking tender care of me as best he could.

"For better or for worse, you, your brothers, Master Larkin and I are simply curiosities to those who have not travelled far, or read many books, because of how we look, of course. The colour of our skin. But with our behaviours we can demonstrate how we are as noble and talented as the very best of gentlemen. The word 'savage' does not apply to us!" and here he roared like a great lion, and my heart bloomed hearing his words, for they weren't spoken in anger or fear, only with a wild pride.

"I performed in front of Queen Victoria herself, once. The best performance in the land. For nearly forty years no one dared suggest I was worth any less than they..." His shoulders slumped a little and he sounded dejected as he added, "A man of colour, they called me in the papers. A coloured gentleman."

110

"Doesn't it bother you?" I whispered, remembering the insults the boys had thrown like stones. "That the colour of our skin is the first thing people see? If they're so blind, how will they ever see anything else?"

"It isn't right, the way they sometimes talk about us, that is true. But, behave like a gentleman and you'll be regarded as one, first and foremost. Circus life knows no colour." He beamed. "Only talent, grit and respect. The horses are also considered wild, but once we agreed to respect one another, they let me command them. That's why I was once the world's best rider. You and George and Lionel have natural ability because *my* blood is *your* blood, and that which runs through us cannot be caged or tamed! We are not designed to sit around reading books; we should be on display, showing people what we can do. That we are champions!"

Surrounded by piles of straw, I lay bleeding and sore on a mattress, and I longed for Mother and blankets, but deep inside, Pablo's words ignited a spark in my soul.

I vowed to make my father proud of me, for *something*. Somehow. I just didn't know for what yet.

"And who's this?" Pablo asked, nodding towards Alma, who was stood by the entrance, toying with the tent flap.

"I'm Alma!"

"Well, come here, girl. Let me look at you. Were you hurt in the skirmish?"

"Oh no, sir, they woulda been lucky to get a hold of me. It was me who chased them away, on account of screaming my head off."

"That's quick thinking. Would you and your family come to the circus this evening, as our guests?"

"I ain't got no family, sir. I'm on me own."

"No family? We all have family, somewhere. Where do you put your head down?"

She sucked at the fingers on her left hand. "I sleeps where I can. It ain't so bad and it's gettin' warmer now. As fer family, well, I runned away from a nasty workhouse. All me family got dead. From the cholera. I'm of a mind to stay here, if you'll have me. I just need a dry place to sleep."

Pablo frowned, but kindly. "We have no space, but I can offer you a warm meal before taking you back to town. Polly will take care of you until the show and fetch you bread and dripping. We'll leave Ted here to rest before he joins you in the audience."

The next time I opened my eyes, Larkin was pacing, sneaking worried glances at me. He frowned, looked like he was about to say something, but changed his mind. "You want anything? Tea maybe?"

All I wanted was answers. Answers as to why this could happen, why people thought they could behave in such a manner. I couldn't look at his face as I asked, "You don't mind then? Being different and standing out?"

He shrugged one-shouldered, offhand. "Why should I?" His tone said otherwise, but perhaps I was mistaken. Maybe he really didn't mind.

"I've just been beaten up because of what I look like! Because of who I am on the outside. But what does the colour of my skin reveal about me? *Nothing!*"

Larkin spat into the sawdust. "Being different is good for business. No one wants to pay to see people they see every day on the street."

He was unquestionably made from stronger stuff than I. For all the hardship he'd encountered – prison, parents dead and years being sent up chimneys – he might as well have been five years older than me, not just a year. Who knows what else he'd seen, or how it had affected him?

Larkin flicked his hand dismissively. "You really think 'William Darby' would get as much attention as 'Pablo Fanque'? Course not!"

"You don't care if people call you lion boy, or 'tinker'?"

"No. I can think of worse."

113

"Like . . . ape noises?"

"Look, if people call us names, it means we got their attention, don't it? If we look exotic, and different, what do you think they'll tell their friends, eh? They'll spread the word that we're something to see. People want to see . . . *wonders*, Ted. To be close to the strange – whether it fascinates or scares them. Whether they like me or loathe me, if they're here, then they ain't ignoring me, are they? It's all the same to us in terms of the money it brings in. Shillings means we get to eat for another day."

My split lip trembled as I remembered how cruel the boys had sounded. "I don't like it."

"The gap between what you don't like and what you can get used to . . . that's a very big one indeed."

I wiped my hand across my face. My voice was small. "I never want anything like that to happen again."

"Better learn to fight then."

"I don't agree with fighting," I croaked, clearing my throat.

"Ever see the boxer Jem Mace?"

"No."

"What those lads done to you today, next time they come callin', you'd best be ready, or you'll end up dead in a ditch. You need to learn how to defend yourself. I'll teach you. Stick your hands up."

"Now? I can hardly move!"

Larkin laughed before moving alongside me. He took my hands and curled them into fists. "We'll have you on your feet before long. In with the other training, I'll show you how to throw a few punches. You won't be riding no horses for a while now anyway, eh?"

He was right. For the first time in a while, I felt a smile start inside me.

14.

After a short rest, I was able to move about a little, though everything ached. My eye was still swollen, and I could only take shallow breaths because my ribs were tender and sore.

In the big tent, by the stables, I found Alma staring up at the horses in wonder.

"The circus will start soon enough," I said.

"Ain't they splendid beasts?" she cried.

I took a breath, carefully. I must be used to the smell of manure now, because I mainly smelt sweet hay.

"They are. I'm only now getting to know them. Pablo's told me lots, but I can't remember all their names, though that one there is Napoleon, and the other Bonaparte."

"What's the difference between a horse 'n a pony?" she asked.

I held my hands wide apart and snickered. "About this much!"

She tutted. "I'm not joking! Have you learnt nothing?"

"I have!"

"Such as?"

"Those three?" I pointed over to a group of horses huddled together. "They're draught horses. They pull our wagons from place to place, but they don't perform. The horses we ride are called resin backs because people put powdered resin on their backs to keep from slipping off – makes for a better grip."

"See? So you *have* learnt things! And how long does it take to train them?"

"The people?"

"No, the horses!"

I thought back to what Pablo and Larkin had told me. "Nine months, Pablo says. Under strict conditions mind you, with experts looking after them."

"What happens if a horse refuses to budge? They're wild, ain't they? I can't imagine they'd listen to what you say, so what do you do then?"

I didn't have any idea but imagined Pablo's voice in my head clear as a bell.

"You have to know your horse. Every horse can become nervous around strange noises, or odd sights.

Maybe he's spotted a shaft of sunlight, or a coat slung over the ring fence, but you give a soothing word and shut the sunbeam out, or remove the coat, and then the horse will be ready to work again."

"How do you get their stuff on them?"

"The best way is not to appear too bothered. Let him see the bridle and sniff at it, so he can tell there's nothing to worry about. Then he'll let you put it over his head. He needs to become used to an audience though; be familiar with hearing laughter and applause and the band."

"Hark at you, Mr Circus Expert!" Alma tapped me good-humouredly on the arm, smiling.

I stepped back. Was she mocking me? But no, seeing her wide smile, I felt warm inside. She was right. I did know something. I'd told *someone else* about the circus. Me, Ted Fanque!

Pablo stood at the entrance to the stables, watching us. "You like what you see, miss?"

She turned to him. "Oh yes! They're wonderful, ain't they? Ted's been tellin' me all about them. I never seen any so close before!"

"Pablo . . ." I ventured. "Alma's got nowhere to go."

"*Someone* will be missing her."

She swung her foot back and forth, kicking into the dirt. "No, they won't." She began sucking her fingers again.

"We can't take in children off the street. I'm sorry, but we aren't a charity."

"Mister, what if I help? I can ... look after the animals and feed them. I sew good, too. Please. I don't eat much. You won't hear a peep; I'll stay out of the way. I never been somewhere like this, it's wonnerful."

"You imagine a circus to be a place of spangles and tinsel and lace; of blaring bands and funny clowns; of beautiful equestriennes and sleek, graceful ponies, of swirling, shimmering beauty? That's only what we want you to see!"

Ever the showman, Pablo pounded a clenched fist into his other hand.

"But! A circus is a machine of gruelling work, of long, hard hours that begin in the grey of dawn and do not cease until the last lamp has been extinguished. The circus fights constantly for its very life. The accidents I've seen over the years! Fire, and flood, and storm. Will you refuse to recognize defeat, even if you encounter it every day? Will you travel, without complaint, in the wind and the rain and the freezing bitter cold?"

"Mister," Alma said, spitting into the mud and wiping her dirty hands down her apron. "Anyone would think you's tryin' to put me off!"

We walked out of the tent with Pablo's booming laugh echoing behind us, to see younger kids running across the field. Brown was by the costume tent and as Alma and I walked towards him, the scamps yelled, "Where are the lions, mister?"

"What do they eat?"

"You, if you're not careful!" he said. He said the same thing at every stop but his answer always seemed fresh and funny. He turned round, thrusting his hands out and roared. Alma squealed with delight and the little ones ran off screaming.

Alma asked, "Have *you* ever seen a lion, Ted?"

"No. Only pictures. Brown, have you seen lions up close?"

Brown was stirring the pot over the fire. "Oh yes! Many times. When I was with Banister and West's, one of his lions was slung in chains over the audience, and one time the chain broke and the beast got free! A girl dashed up and grabbed it by the mane – just like that!"

"Was she ripped to shreds?" I asked, my hand over my mouth.

"That's what we *thought* would happen ... He was a particularly savage animal who'd nipped his trainer more than once, but the ringmaster said to the girl gently, 'That's right, dear, stand as you are, perfectly still.'"

"Why didn't he tell her to run?"

"He knew the slightest movement would be a

calamity. They cleared the house and enticed the lion away, but had difficulty in netting the creature."

Alma was wide-eyed. "No one was hurt?"

"Wouldn't be much of a clown if I filled your heads with stories of maulings and deaths, eh? When it was over, the ringmaster asked her, 'Dear, whatever gave you the courage?' and she said, 'Oh, that was nothing, it was just like a big dog.'" Brown laughed. "Imagine that! 'A big dog'!"

A loud deep bell rang.

"The start of the show!" Brown announced. "Better get ready!" He hurried towards the large tent.

15.

Alma and I followed behind him. Pablo had said we could both watch the show, but we should squeeze close together and not take up too much room.

The atmosphere was bustling. The hired band played, while the audience filed in and took their seats, chattering. The ring, full of sawdust, was cordoned off by rope and the glare of gas lamps, hanging from tent poles, created a hazy gentle glow all around.

"What's that nice smell?" Alma asked, crinkling her nose, as we shuffled along one of the benches at the back. "It's stinging my nostrils!"

"Oranges. People buy them during the show," I replied, pointing to Clara dressed up, selling them from a tray, moving through the audience.

Alma's eyes widened seeing children tearing off the peel and slurping the juice. "I've never had one!"

Brown, now dressed in red-and-white-striped

trousers and a baggy, floppy coat, stood in the centre of the ring. He stretched his arms out, much like that first morning I'd met him, and addressed the crowd in a voice brimming with laughter.

He twirled his hat and danced a little jig. "We have . . . dishes to please old and young, father and son, daughter and mother, sister and brother! Whether you are fat or lean, dirty or clean, short and small or big and tall. You might be wise and witty, or ugly or pretty. We don't care if you're good or bad, simple or sad, once you're in our tent, then you'll see no precedent!"

"I have never seen the circus." Alma's face was lit up with wonder. Despite my memories of Aston Park, tingles were in my tummy too. I'd seen everyone rehearsing but somehow, even after all this time, I'd not watched an entire show. Sometimes I pretended to, but then crept out, and at other times I was on box office, taking the money. Most times I was kept busy helping behind the curtain.

Pablo, as the ringmaster, tramped into the ring. His white gloves shone and he held two whips in either hand, a long one with a tapering lash, and a slender, thinner switch. Cracking them, he twirled both above his head.

Thudding unseen hooves gave us a start and burst into view. Cymbals crashed, bells jangled and a troupe of eight horses cantered out, their coats shiny like satin. Colourful feathers were stuck on to their harnesses.

Pablo's whips never touched the horses, but as his lips moved, the horses stood with their forelegs up on brightly painted tubs. Then they bent low on bended knees, bowing to their king!

Powerful and massive, they towered over Pablo, reminding us of who was in charge here. How brave he was, doing this for over thirty years, twice a day, every day. Is this what the world would expect from me, because I was his son? Is this what Lionel had done before running off?

The horses cantered round, following Pablo's every lash whip, harnesses jangling. Then they moved sideways into the shape of a star, and were so obedient it was as if they were under a spell.

Clara whirled past on one of the horses, crouched next to its flowing black mane. The other horses stood still in formation.

A man dressed as an army general gave a war-cry, clear above the band. He held up a hoop covered over with tissue paper. Clara raced round the ring, towards the hoop, and then crashed through, leaping through it, tearing the tissue in two. The horse raced beneath it and Clara landed perfectly upon her horse again. Thunderous applause and the audience rose to their feet.

Brayed in by trumpets, Polly swung into the arena next. With a bound, she stood astride two horses, one foot upon each, and with their necks arched, snorting nostrils and heads shaking, they thundered around the ring like gods. She jumped on to one and turned a pirouette on the horse's back.

My soul sped round with Polly. I was spellbound but terrified. Seeing Polly in rehearsals felt very different to being here with the music and roaring crowd. What if Polly or Clara fell? Surely they would be trampled to death under those powerful hooves and iron shoes. They were travelling faster than locomotives!

Ostrich feathers were atop Polly's head and the colours caught the glow of the lamps and sparkled. The audience hushed, and all we heard were intakes of breath.

They seemed so happy and free in the ring. I suddenly understood the appeal and why Pablo hadn't wanted to leave this behind. If someone experienced this glamour every day, why would they want to be cooped up in a place so dull as a house, or to work day after day in a mill, or a factory, or a mine? How tired, cold and boring everything but the circus seemed now!

Alma elbowed me. "That's the most beautiful thing I've ever seen."

I sighed. "I know."

Alma sputtered, laughing. "*I'm* talking about the horse, are you?"

Colour rushed into my cheeks.

Next, Brown tripped up and fell flat and we laughed and laughed. Brown certainly knew how to crack a wheeze; jokes and puns tumbled easily from his lips. Then he climbed a ladder, stood on his head on the top rung, and in that position drank a glass of wine! When he was safely on the ground again, he performed silly dances and my heart ached, thinking of George and Mother and the instances when George and I made each other laugh, often at those moments when we weren't supposed to. I wished they could both see this.

The tumbling Bellinis came on next. They juggled and tumbled with balls, oranges and knives. I scrunched up my face and twisted away, my stomach clenching tight, fearing one of them might fall. But they didn't. As they took their bows, Alma jumped up.

"I needs the privy!" She shuffled past me, out of the tent.

A group of ponies trotted out into the middle of the ring. One pony gave us a wave with his right foot and bowed his head, then they did a three-legged gallop by sticking their legs out in a straight line.

Such clever animals! No wonder Pablo adored them. They fought, they leapt over poles and through hoops, they sat down and stood up on command, all whilst wearing cloaks and lace caps. They sat at a table, as if being served a meal, and they fetched and carried. I almost died laughing when they played leapfrog.

"Next, a daring act of horsemanship. Master Larkin on his bare-backed steed!"

Larkin came out wearing a peacock's tail feather stuck in a headband, perched jauntily on his head. He clung with his arms and legs to the horse's neck. He seemed to me nothing less than a length of elastic, he moved and stretched so easily. He stood and leapt backwards and forwards, turning and twisting, weaving like a giant snake.

As Larkin left the ring, he leaned, smiling, over the horse, and careered past Polly, who jumped on to his horse along with him, her hair flowing down her back like waves. They threw a kiss to the audience amidst cheers and gasps.

Alma squeezed her way past me, wiping orange pips from her face. "What did I miss?"

"The ponies."

I didn't remember anything as grand as this from my circus visit before. Perhaps seeing the woman fall, with all that panic, had crowded out everything else.

The show didn't end there. Larkin and Polly had been only a warm-up. The real star of the show charged in – my father! He rode round the ring, twice the speed of the others, galloping so fast he was a blur.

Alma said, "Why's he not face down, snorting sawdust?"

With his foot on Bessie's head and the other foot up on her shoulder, they leant together. He and that horse were part of each other. I couldn't see where he ended and Bessie began. How was he still upright and not being trampled to death? What held him up? It had to be a force of nature greater than any known before.

Pablo was transformed in front of my very eyes! Watching him, my stomach swelled with pride, as if a flock of birds beat their wings inside my chest. He looked so elegant and . . . natural with those horses. I was witnessing a man at the top of his profession, an expert.

Maybe those bullies had done me a favour. Although I didn't know if I'd ever be as talented as Pablo, as he made every move look effortless and easy, I wanted to try. Maybe his circus spirit had been passed down to me. Perhaps there was still time to discover what I was good at?

Of course I wanted to see Mother and George, and be back home, but I also wanted this man – Pablo – to be proud of me. The way he'd cared for me, and spoken out with such pride and passion, I wanted to see his face light up with the same bright grin he flashed so often at Larkin.

I longed for Pablo to say, 'Well done, Ted!'

Pablo had hired a woman temporarily to walk the tightrope. Larkin explained the tightrope was always a big draw but that she could only stay for a few performances. The rope was raised off the ground – so high that I needed to squint – and from this position, it didn't look very thick; certainly not thick enough to hold a person. My hands started to feel clammy so I wiped them along my trousers. This brought it all back – when I'd seen that woman fall. I stared upwards and from this distance, the two women even looked the same with their long dark tresses and white costume.

Part of me wanted to leave, but deep down, I suspected if I didn't watch this now then I would always be afraid of the tightrope. I needed to face my fears, little by little.

She held her arms out to the side with wicker baskets on her hands and alternated between walking and then running across the rope.

"She's copying Blondin," I said to Alma, keen to show my knowledge of famous performers Larkin had told me about.

"Who?"

"In America, a man called Blondin crossed Niagara

Falls on the rope. It was in the *Illustrated London News*."

"What in heavens for?" She creased her face up, looking scornful.

"Not just that – he did other things too: cooked an omelette, went across blindfolded *and* on stilts, and even carried his manager across the falls on his back!"

"Who would want to do that?"

"Whoever wants to be famous, I guess. Those who want to . . . be remembered."

"Pfft. There is better ways to be 'membered than being dead, it seems to me."

I glanced back up at the walker – she'd stopped moving and was wobbling. My heart lurched into my throat. Was she going to fall? Was I about to witness another death?

16.

The sky was black, except for the shimmering pinpricks of stars. It was past ten 'o clock but the night was fresh and bright. The last of the audience left the field, babbling amongst themselves.

I was the happiest I'd been since Pablo had brought me here. I inhaled a cool spring breath, gazing at the vast starry sky. The breath filled my lungs and then I let all the air out of my nostrils in a *whoosh*. I had stayed to watch the tightrope walker. I had stayed to watch, with my eyes open, and she'd not fallen. No one had died tonight. Things were changing, I could feel it.

Next to a wagon, Alma and I stood listening to Larkin, Polly, Edwin and Clara discussing their performances; what had gone well and what they'd do differently next time.

But then an anguished roar, man not beast, came from inside the smaller tent.

"Where is it?" Pablo flew out of the tent, his clothes rumpled and his hat askew. "Who *dares* to steal from me?" His eyes were wild with fury. "Thirty pounds – gone!"

Everyone rushed over. All I heard were raised voices.

Brown twisted his hands in front of him and said to me, in low tones, "This has happened before. The night his first wife, Susannah, died. The evening's takings, more than fifty pounds, stolen amid the pandemonium."

And tonight, thirty pounds? With twenty shillings to the pound and me earning two shillings a week from the steel factory – that was the equivalent of nearly six years' wages!

Alma started sucking her fingers, watching Pablo, Larkin, Clara and Polly all disappear into the small tent.

I asked, "What shall we do?"

"There's not much you *can* do, m'boy," Brown said. "Get yourself to bed and I'll see what's happening. Clara was on box office; perhaps she didn't lock the takings box. If so there'll be hell to pay. Best stay out of the way. We might have to ride into town for the police, I don't know yet."

"Mister?"

We both looked down at Alma, who was looking very small and cold.

"Yes, m'dear?" Brown said kindly.

"I'm tired. Pablo said he would take me to town but ... would ya mind if I stayed here tonight?"

"That will be fine. I'll fetch Polly and she'll take you to the sleeping tent."

The atmosphere of joy had changed to one of consternation. There was nothing to do but try to sleep too.

It was difficult to settle; not only was I bruised, but dismayed too, knowing that there might be a thief amongst us. I tossed and turned, unable to make myself comfortable on the piles of straw and blankets, due to my injuries as well as my mind churning over the evening's events. The thief had to be an audience member, didn't it? Someone who'd come late and seen the flap of the tent open?

I flicked through *Varney*, but my eyes were too sore to read. I picked up my kaleidoscope and cradled it to me, thinking of home and Mother and George. Wishing I was with them.

I woke with a start. Heard rustling. I blearily opened my eyes to see Larkin's face lit up by the lamp he held. No one else was in bed yet. I expected the Bellini brothers and Brown were with Pablo, searching for the culprit.

I don't know if it was the rustling, or the fact I'd woken so suddenly, but I spoke before I had a chance to consider my words.

"Was it you?" I whispered.

Larkin gave a start, seeing me sat upright. "Me?"

"Be a gentleman. Did you take the money?"

He turned his back on me. "You bleedin' mad?"

"It strikes me that someone like you could do very well on thirty pounds, if you were of a mind to know where to hide it."

Larkin span round, his eyes narrowed. "Someone . . . 'like me'?" His jaw was set hard, the muscles in his cheekbones twitching and flexing.

"You've been in prison before . . . for stealing." His look was so furious that I recoiled slightly. "By your own admission," I added, defensively. "Not to mention seeing you steal food with my own eyes!"

"You always jump to the worst conclusions about me. I don't know why. Are you jealous? Open your eyes, Ted. I have no need to steal money. I have everything I want here. I think of this as my family – *unlike some*."

My tone was emotionless. "You ought to confess to Pablo, before the police arrive."

"You'd like that, wouldn't you? Then you'd have Pablo all to yourself. That what you want? Maybe *you* took it and are setting me up!" His tone was the stoniest

I'd ever heard. Cold, with layers of hurt threaded through, like frost.

By now, both of us were stood facing each other. Our voices were raised enough to draw the attention of the Bellini brothers, smoking outside, because they came in and put themselves between us.

"Don't argue!" Hugo implored.

Edwin put his palms on each of our chests. "Friends! Friends!" he said. "What is this?"

"The circus. We stick together," Sid cried, passionately. "We are as one."

Larkin and I were so het up that we both dashed Edwin's hands away. I didn't wish to be calmed; didn't want to forget how my blood throbbed, boiling in my veins. If it was indeed Larkin who had stolen, then he shouldn't be permitted to get away with this.

"Away, boys." Larkin stepped back from Edwin and spat on to the ground. "Let us talk."

"There was about to be a good deal more 'n talking," Hugo butted in.

"We got things to straighten out and it ain't your place to interfere, right?" Larkin said, firmly. The brothers backed off, tacitly nodding their understanding.

Larkin watched them leave the tent before turning to me. "Pablo don't need you, you know."

"Pardon?"

"He don't *need* you. He just *wants* you here. *I* often wants things, but all I *need* is a dry place to sleep, food and water. Everything else is extra. Sooner or later, Pablo will realize that what he wants ain't good for what his business needs. He'll come to his senses, see that you add nothing of value and chuck you out on your ear."

I stood firm. "He won't."

"He will. His pockets ain't limitless. 'Specially when people are stealing from him."

"But . . . he can't . . . I'm his son," I faltered, realizing that I no longer wanted to be sent home.

"So? He was happy enough without you all this time. . ."

"Well, *he* was the one to fuss and bring me here!"

"When *he* wanted to. You said yourself, he never bothered before now, did he? Ever stop to wonder why?"

I swallowed hard against the rush of tears choking my throat. "I didn't even want to come! It stinks! I hate it and you're a bunch of show-offs. I want no part of it!"

Larkin looked like he'd won a prize. "That's just as well then, 'cos none of us want any part of you neither!"

He grabbed my kaleidoscope from my bed and hurled it across the tent. Silence slapped me as it struck the tent pole in the centre. The side of it caved in and

138

mirror fragments flew everywhere.

I couldn't move. I stared at the broken pieces of my most precious thing.

Larkin's cheeks were high with colour and his voice had lost its mocking air.

"I weren't thinking, Ted. I didn't mean to ... I didn't mean to ... *break it*."

If I'd been a boy who believed in using his fists, I would have struck Larkin, but instead I used my words, which I knew from fights with George often hurt deeper and held a longer lasting pain.

I said, icily, "I wouldn't have expected anything else from a thief. You're the very definition of a *savage*, aren't you?"

I walked stiffly towards the buckled tube and, trying to conceal how much I trembled, crouched to gather it up. As I did so, I tried *not* to think of the day Mother had given it to me. Tried to forget her expression as I unwrapped the package and how, seeing me so happy, her eyes had misted over. I tried, I really did, with every fibre of my heart, to forget how, the second I'd held the tube up to look through it for the first time, my breath had been sucked out of me as, mesmerized, I watched the glass inside tumble and fall in beautiful broken shards, creating complicated, magical, inexplicable patterns.

"I didn't mean it! I mean—"

I whirled round to face Larkin, my anger coalescing into a scorching coal of darkness.

"My *mother* gave that to me!" As I shrieked, and my voice splintered on the word 'mother', I understood that Larkin had shattered much more than glass and crumpled much more than tin. The warped kaleidoscope was nothing more than a hollow tube with useless unconnected bits rattling round inside it – and now, I was the same.

I tried to tell myself that this toy, this ... *trinket* ... wasn't important. That I was looking at nothing but glass and mirrors and illusions, that I was, in fact, too old for such things, but I couldn't do it.

All I wanted was Mother, my brother and my bed. How had I nearly convinced myself that this place, noisy and busy, could ever become a place where I felt comfortable or accepted, or would wish to call home?

I fell to my knees, fighting back sobs, and hoped against hope that when I turned around again Larkin would be gone.

17.

Halfway crossing the field, still riled up from my fight with Larkin and the night's drama, I didn't notice Polly emerge from the shadows of the big tent.

"What are you doing awake?" She sounded surprised.

"Same could be asked about you," I retorted, peeved at finding someone else out here. Sometimes when I couldn't sleep, I'd taken to visiting the ponies. Often, I'd see Pablo leaving the stables. I'd wait till he was gone because I didn't always want to hear stories of him and his glory. Sometimes, I wanted to be alone. To see if I could get to know the horses' personalities in my own time.

Polly said, "It is a nice night to consider the stars. All that horrid business this evening, after such a wonderful performance – it fair riled me up."

I rubbed my forehead. "Isn't that right." I wondered if she knew about Larkin's prison history.

She sidled alongside me, looking me steadily in the eyes. "Who do you think stole from us?"

"I don't know." I felt strangely guilty, even though I knew nothing about the missing money. "What about you?"

"I'm no thief!" She slapped a hand across her mouth, shocked.

"N-no," I stuttered. "I meant, who do *you* fancy for it?"

She pursed her lips, thinking. "Oh, an audience member who chanced it – has to be. We've all known each other for months, some of us for *years*, and nothing like this has happened before. The only *new* faces are you and your pal. And, though it ain't for me to say, I doubt it's either of you. Else it'd make no sense you still hanging round, for one thing, unless you're lacking in the brains department!" She laughed hard.

"It's not me," I said, wearily. "Polly . . . can I ask you something?"

"Course."

"Do *you* think Pablo wants me around, or am I just . . . cheap labour?"

"What a question, Master Ted! Who has put such doubt into that young head of yours?"

I shrugged. "Just something Larkin said."

She waved her hand, dismissively. "Oh, don't mind

him. Likes to wag his tongue, that one. His nose is out of joint 'cos once you've settled in and learnt our ways you might discover you can do all sorts. He's probably worried you'll put him to shame!"

"Did you know Lionel?"

"No. I'm not *that* old! Brown knew him. Your father is pleased you're here, don't doubt it. He's a good man; one of the most respected circus owners around these parts."

I didn't care about that right now. Maybe Larkin was correct, Pablo wasn't interested in raising a son; probably only wanted one to carry on his name and tell stories to.

Polly took my hand and gently led me to the steps of a wagon and indicated I should sit down. She pulled her shawl close around her shoulders. "Pablo's not one of them men who only does things to be thought of as noble; he puts his money where his mouth is. He's a member of the Ancient Shepherds."

"What's that?" I asked.

"They help families down on their luck. He puts on benefits for circus folk who've been loyal and worked hard. Like, if their families ain't got much money, or someone gets ill, or dies ... their burial has to be paid for, don't it? Pablo raises money for them. And *that's* the real reason his circus is still going. Why we stick by him even though we ain't seen any wages lately. He creates goodwill. His reputation is positive 'cos he works twice as hard as anyone else. You're lucky to belong to Pablo's circus."

"Is that why you're here? He helped your family?"

She shook her head. "No. I've been his apprentice since I was eight."

"You're very talented; if there are bigger, better circuses where you could earn more, why do you stay?"

"Because Pablo treats me like a daughter, not an employee. And I stay for the courage I see displayed every day. Here, the impossible becomes . . . *possible*. At my first circus, I heard an acrobat say, 'No matter what happens in my life – I have lived more than anyone else.' What he said stirred something inside me, and I've been in love with the circus ever since. Now, it's really very late. *I'm* heading back to sleep and you should too."

I watched Polly cross the field and go into her own sleeping tent.

When I entered the stables, a small figure with its back to me was untying one of the ponies.

"Who's there?" I said, squinting, puffing up my voice in case someone was stealing more than just the takings.

I moved closer and my blood stopped cold in my veins. "*Alma?*" I whispered, narrowing my eyes, able to make out her balancing on an upturned crate, trying to climb on to one of the smaller ponies. "What are you doing?"

She kept jumping, trying her damnedest to mount the thing. "What does it look like?" she sniffled. "I gots to *go*!"

"It's no time to be riding, that's for sure," I joked, even though there was no mistaking what was going on, no other conclusion to reach except she was stealing a pony.

"Where are you going?"

She finally got on to the pony. Her little face was blotchy and red from crying, but her chin jutted out. She looked directly at me.

"I lied 'bout having no family." She bit her lip. "Me, Ma and Pa and five – three – *three* sisters ... is all in the spike."

"*Prison?*"

She frowned. "No! Not prison! The *workhouse*. I got out. But I got to get back, give the master this money. Then maybe he'll help us get lodgings, or find work, if I offers him money while I figure out what to do."

"*You* stole from us?" I whispered, barely registering I'd said 'us', that I already considered myself part of this circus.

She nodded, flushing. "My family ... they're *sick*," she whimpered. "Everyone is so sick."

"A likely story!" I shouted. "Three sisters or five? Which of your lies can't you keep straight?"

I couldn't believe I'd fallen for her sweet caring act, down by the river, when obviously this had been her plan all along! Perhaps she belonged to a child gang, like in the story of *Oliver Twist* that I'd heard about.

She looked mortified. "I *had* five, but two died, one in me very arms, and nows I only got three left!" She wailed, loud enough to wake people sleeping the other side of town. She stuck her fingers in her mouth and sucked on them hard, hiccupping at the same time.

One glance at her tears and I knew I'd gone too far. Of course she was telling the truth. I gathered my thoughts while she quietened, still slurping on her fingers.

I stepped towards her. I put my hand on the pony's head, and softly said, "But, Alma, that money isn't yours. *You* know that. That's people's wages. You've seen how hard they work."

"I was hoping to be gone! B-b-but *you*, and now. . ." She started bawling again and then slumped over the pony, letting the reins slacken.

I stroked the pony's mane and put my other hand lightly on Alma's back.

"I'm very sorry about your sisters. I miss George and my mother every day. Part of me would like to run off with you, but I can't disappoint my mother. I don't think that you can go back to the workhouse now, either. You might get put in prison yourself if you turn up with thirty pounds. Please, stay here."

She sobbed in earnest then, wept and wept, her little body convulsing.

"I can't let you run away with Pablo's takings, Alma. Come on down now. Let us go to him."

18.

Alma rubbed frantically at her face, frowning. "You could just put it back! No one would need know."

"But Pablo might be able to help you. Polly says he helps people that need it, but only if we're honest and explain."

"Can't we wait till morning?" she asked.

"No, I don't think so," I replied, kindly. I helped her down off the pony and we led it back to its stall.

We walked quietly across the field to Pablo's living wagon. Alma was shivering and sniffling, and I was a little nervous at what Pablo's reaction might be – would he have her arrested? Beat her? Blame me for bringing her here? – but I also suspected that we were doing the proper thing.

We knocked on the tin side of the wagon. Eventually, Pablo poked his head out, bleary-eyed. His black fuzzy hair stood on end, giving him a slightly comical appearance, and I smiled, despite the grave situation.

He rubbed at his face. "Is it the horses?" he asked, squinting.

"No, sir. Nothing like that to worry about."

"What then?" He was annoyed. "I was in a deep slumber!"

I spoke quickly, "Alma here ... has something to say." I put my hand on her shoulder and urged her forward.

Pablo glared at us. "Well?"

Alma twisted her thin scratched hands, staring at the ground. "It was me that took your money, sir." She grimaced, swallowed and faced him square on.

"WHAT?" Pablo gripped the side of the wagon. "*You*? Where is my thirty pounds?"

She was visibly trembling. "Here." She handed him a purse from deep in her apron. He snatched it off her and rifled through it, counting.

Satisfied, he shoved the money in his pocket. He rubbed both hands wearily over his face, pulling at his whiskers.

We waited, but he just stood there, staring at the empty purse in his hand. Eventually, he handed it back to Alma.

"You see something of England, after thirty years

of travelling *every day* from March to October. Every weather and type of road – and you get a measure of people too. Over the years, me and Brown have spent all night searching for horses who've escaped the field; we've tramped for miles in rain and darkness."

His voice cracked, despite its sharp edge. I had no idea what he was talking about, but Alma and I listened dutifully.

"Setting up the tents in cold weather, we've nearly frozen to death, and almost suffocated in the summer, when the air is stifling. I've been so hard up I've walked twenty miles to save a fare. Been so tired I've fallen asleep standing up."

Alma moved to speak, but Pablo held up his hand and glared. I'd never seen him look this angry.

His voice was commanding. "I have faced many *many* people who hate the circus. Fools who think my horses are trained by cruelty. Men have called me names on account of my skin. It took me longer than most to rise to the top – that much is true. I was forty before I could branch out on my own, half my life already behind me. Left Batty's circus with only two horses! *Two.* I have worked harder than any man alive in order to create this life for myself. What wickedness to steal from me!"

"I'm so sorry!" Alma cried. She threw herself

forward on to her knees, arms thrust out pleading. "It was – it's my family, sir! Please – don't beat me!"

"You said you had no family!" Pablo roared, still annoyed.

I reached for Alma's hand and squeezed it, helping her up. "Alma, tell him. *Please*."

She explained about her family being in the workhouse. Pablo listened to her sobbing for a full ten minutes and didn't interrupt, but he didn't offer any comfort or reassurance either. I couldn't believe how mistreated she'd been.

"Alma," he said, sternly. "Theft is unacceptable. If I cannot trust my circus members, we're doomed. You will obviously need to stay with us now in order to work off your debt, and we will be watching you carefully."

She snorted back snot and snuffled, becoming quiet. Did she know that he was making sure she'd have somewhere safe to stay? That he'd made it sound like he was punishing her, but actually wasn't at all!

Pablo's expression softened. "I understand about the workhouse. More than you know." He sounded drained. "I myself have unpleasant memories of my days in that terrible place." His eyes clouded over suddenly, as if a candle had been snuffed out.

He coughed. "You both need a good night's sleep,

but I promise, come morning light I'll ride to Ripon and visit your family. Now, rest. You're lucky tomorrow isn't a pull-down day."

And with that he banged the door to his wagon shut.

19.

The next morning, Pablo was as good as his word. After we'd eaten breakfast, he rode off to see Alma's family. She begged to ride with him, but he said Ripon would be a day's journey, and it'd be faster if he went alone. Besides, he added, if the master or matron caught sight of her, they might insist she return. After all, she had the uniform they'd issued, so technically it belonged to them; who knew how they'd respond to *that* theft?

Pablo had explained to the troupe that the takings had been found, but had said nothing more about it, even when pressed.

A few of us stood around the cooking pot, which was the warmest place to be first thing in the morning and last thing at night.

"I wasn't *born* in no workhouse," Alma said, after Pablo had told everyone where he was going. "Ma and me used to sell flowers and Pa was a wheelwright, but his hand got mangled up somethin' dreadful." She screwed up her face.

"How long were you in the workhouse?" I asked, supping my tea.

She counted on her fingers. "Since I were about seven. So, four years."

"The workhouse must have been horrible!" Polly exclaimed.

Alma sighed. "It was, but there were no point cryin' over it. The porridge was slop – more water than oatmeal, with black bits in it; we saw 'em squirmin'!"

Polly handed me a bowl of broth and a hunk of bread, and said quietly in my ear, as she took my empty cup, "Got some apologizing to do then, have you, Master Ted?"

Gulp. Larkin must have told her that I had accused him. Why had I jumped to such conclusions? I'd hardly treated him fairly.

"This is delicious!" Alma said, gobbling up her broth.

Polly beamed. "It ain't nothing but some soup thickened with barley, but I'm glad you like it. Back to rehearsing as usual then," she said, wiping her mouth. "Alma, it's time Clara and I taught you how to earn your keep – that's *if* you're staying, which I take it you are?"

"Course!" Alma lifted the bowl and slurped the rest into her mouth. "I can't do no tricks though."

Polly tutted. "There's more ways to be of use other than performing. Takes an army to run things properly around here. Come on, we'll start with fixing up the horses."

Wistfully, I watched Alma and Polly cross the field to the big tent. With no Pablo or Alma to distract me, that left only rehearsals and . . . Larkin.

I still needed to find something I was good at. With money scarce back home . . . well, I'd never be sending home much, or have a circus life for long, if I couldn't find my talent. And what if I didn't have one? What if there was nothing I was good at? What if I couldn't ride a horse, or balance, or juggle a ball? What would become of me then?

Larkin emerged from the sleeping tent and ignored me so blatantly I was shamefaced. He grabbed himself a slice of bread and smeared it with dripping.

I moved alongside him. "I'm sorry," I said.

He didn't look me in the eye. "What for?"

I lowered my voice because Hugo and Sid, standing next to a wagon the other side of the cooking pot, were both listening in, and pretending not to. "You *know* what for."

Larkin didn't smile. He said, callously, "Maybe I

do, and maybe I don't. Maybe I want to hear you say it. Maybe I reckon you should squirm, so you have some idea of what that feels like."

"All right!" I grabbed a hunk of bread and swiped it round my broth bowl. "All right. I shouldn't have accused you of stealing the takings."

"You remember what you said, hm? Remember what you called me?"

I nodded and stared at the ground. My voice was as small as I felt. "I do."

"Well?"

I cried, "I'm sorry for that 'n' all. I'm *sorry*! What about you breaking *my* things!"

"Well, *you* broke my . . . feelings. Enough. Apology accepted." He bent over and grabbed three bread rolls from the dish in front of the cooking pot. "There's practice to do. Still gotta find you something to be good at. Gotta earn your keep."

"*I* haven't seen any wages yet."

"That's 'cos he ain't seen nothing worthy from you. You gotta prove yourself as an investment first, ain't ya?" He pressed one of the rolls into my hand. "Don't eat that."

He was forgiving me already? I followed him over to an empty space.

"Right," Larkin commanded. "Juggling. The

basics. Let's see if you can catch, to begin with. Face me. You've a bread roll in your right hand. Now, I'm your partner, see? Throw that to me – no, not *yet*! I'll catch it with my *left* hand, throw it into my own right hand, and then back to you. Catch it with *your* left hand. Understand?"

"I think so," I said, stiffly. No, he was definitely still smarting.

"We carry on doing that until the move is smooth and practised without us dropping any."

We threw the bread roll to each other a few times, back and forth, but before I knew it, he was hurling them hard and fast at my head, with no intention of juggling at all!

"You think a 'sorry' is good enough?"

Ducking and dodging from the bread rolls flying my way, I yelled, "How else am I to make things right?"

"I haven't thought about it. But ... maybe your stinking apology ain't enough. Maybe my time here is done. Maybe I'll be moving on."

He stalked off towards the circus tent. Although Pablo had been decent enough to not name Alma as the thief, I wanted to let Larkin know who had actually stolen the money; I owed him that much. I sprinted across the field and caught up to him. I touched his elbow lightly.

"Don't go."

He span round, startled. "What do you care?" He spat into the grass, very near to my boot.

"I do care! Who else will ..." *Understand what it's like to be me?* I nearly said, but instead all that came out was, " ...teach me to tumble and juggle? Please, Larkin. Don't leave. There's space for us both."

"I ain't seen you making much effort, even though you keep saying you're trying."

"I nearly got thrown the other day. Not been on a horse since. Anyway, after the ... well, my ribs still ache, you know?"

"Ah." He nodded slowly, as if he knew something that I didn't. "Right. What about ... balancing things, like we talked about?"

"I tried balancing something light in my palm, but I couldn't move it to the back of my hand. Kept falling off. I tried for ages."

Larkin peered at me. "How many times did you try?"

"A few."

"Really? Look," He dug out a shilling from his pocket and put it in his palm, then tossed it into the air, catching it on the back of his hand. Then he did the same thing with another shilling, both hands at the same time. How did he do that?

"Slowly move the things up your arm and on to the elbow. It'll teach you how to keep balance."

"What'll Pablo do if I don't find any talent, if there's nothing I can do and I end up being … just another mouth to feed?"

Larkin shrugged. "You've less appetite than the last permanent fixture."

"I'm serious! It'll be a waste, won't it? Me being here if I can't do nothing."

"It's not as if you're here to save the circus – how could you? We all know business is tough. But you bring the Fanque name with you and *that's* what he wants: a good enough reason to draw the crowds. *Pablo's Family Circus* … well, without you there ain't much 'family', is there?"

Larkin was right. Pablo wasn't going to give up on me; he wasn't going to stop trying.

"Ted, you still don't *want* to be here, do you? You've no intention of trying to learn!"

"That's not true!" I retorted.

"Course it is!" Larkin turned a somersault. "Aha! *Now* everything makes sense … Why you're always so keen to clean or help Polly cook. Anything rather than get on them horses."

"I *have* been practising! I stretch all the time, just like you told me to."

"Says you."

"*Yes*, says I!"

Larkin had it wrong. I *did* want to be a part of the circus. I wanted to make Pablo proud. I wanted to earn my keep, send home money to Mother so she didn't have to take in mending, and help contribute to George's medicine; I just didn't know how to do it, that was all, and it seemed time was running out.

20.

I was pleased, and slightly relieved, when Pablo returned to the grounds later, trotting slowly on a stumbling, exhausted-looking Bessie.

"She's fair worn out," he said, dismounting. "Here, Larkin! Help me take her to the stables and get her some water. We both need a feed."

"Did you not stop at an inn?" Larkin asked, coming over and nuzzling into Bessie's mane.

I held back till Pablo noticed me.

"No inn, not tonight," he said. "Don't worry, Ted. I'll find little Alma in a while and give her the news."

"What news might that be?" I asked.

He frowned, shaking his head. "No immediate solution presents itself. Alma's mother has many mouths to feed; it isn't the proper time to leave the workhouse. However, I took them out for a hearty supper and promised that in a week or so, I would return and see what could be done."

Larkin narrowed his eyes at Pablo. "You can afford to be so generous?"

"Watch your tongue!" Pablo snapped, whirling round. "How I conduct my affairs is not your concern."

Larkin grumbled under his breath. "It is when we ain't been paid for weeks." He pressed his lips tightly together.

"Yet do you want for anything?" Pablo demanded. He took off his hat and wiped at his forehead with a handkerchief.

Larkin scuffed his boot back and forth, kicking up mud. "If you don't want me here anymore, just say it." With a jerk of his thumb, he indicated me behind him. "You brought him in to replace me, right?"

"Don't be a fool." Pablo began to smile and then stopped himself. "There's room for us all!"

"Tosh! Ted thought *I* was the one who stole your money! Why should I stay somewhere I ain't wanted?"

Pablo held Bessie by the lead rein, taking her toward the big tent and the stables. "Come, Larkin. No one thinks that. I've plans. Didn't you say you had new tricks? Don't be offended, I've enough worries without needing to replace my best rider."

Larkin's face relaxed and a smile emerged. "Your best?"

"Of course."

Larkin thought for a moment. "I don't mind waiting for our wages, you know I don't, but the others—"

"I know, I know," Pablo bit his lip. He pulled sharply at the cuffs on his overcoat. "I appreciate your loyalty, my boy." He lowered his voice, and moved closer to Larkin, although I could still hear. "I am trying to fix it. I just need a little … more *time*."

Later, after Alma and I had finished a game of marbles and fed the ponies, we wandered over to the big top. Both of us were surprised to see Larkin halfway up the ladder leading to the wooden platform where the high-wire performers usually stood.

"What are you doing up there?" Alma called out.

He paused with his back to us, before turning around and yelling down, "Pablo ain't let me get up here, but I can do it. He knows I can. Galloping horses is a rush, but up here is something else, being so high, seeing all them people so small. No one can touch you. I got to make Pablo realize he ain't seen the best of me yet. I got more to give."

Alma stood underneath the rope. "You'll be givin' him funeral costs if you ain't careful."

I craned my neck; he was about halfway up, a good giraffe height, at least. "Alma's talking sense. What if you have an accident?"

"What if?" Larkin jeered. "What if you wake up dead tomorrow, hm?"

"Then you'd scarcely be waking up, would you?" I snapped. "Larkin! Pablo already said you were the best."

He stopped climbing and came down. Once he was on solid ground I tried to smooth things over. "No matter how many years I train, I could never do what you do."

"Yeah." He smiled, sheepishly. "I've seen you around the horses – not exactly a natural."

Alma stepped up. "Not everyone is made to ride horses." She practically bared her teeth at Larkin.

Larkin mused, "The thing is ... people are *used to* horses. Our show needs something new – different. I seen this act in Brown's paper, about this fella who made a big splash by sticking rubber pads to his feet and walking along a plank."

"What's so new about that?" Alma scoffed.

"The plank was stuck to the ceiling," Larkin replied. "*And* he was hung upside down!"

I thought back to Brown's papers scattered round the sleeping tent. "I saw that too. The man *died*."

Larkin waved his hands as if I was a killjoy. "Pfft."

"He *died*, Larkin."

"He only died 'cos the plaster gave way."

"Exactly, so it's not a *safe* trick, is it?"

"Since when is the circus *safe*? Everything has risk, or should do! Why do you think people come?"

Alma hollered, "Stop it!" She sniffed, gulping back tears. "I thought this was a *family* . . . I thought you two was *friends*."

Larkin griped, "Sometimes we're friends, and sometimes we're not."

"You squabble just like me and my sisters!" Alma said. "Use your noggin, Larkin. You can't do that plank trick because there's nothing to hold you up."

"I know. I'm thinking of that trick for when we're back in buildings, during winter. For now, I got something else. I been practising."

He dashed behind the curtain separating the ring from the acts about to come on. Then, two-handed, he rolled out a massive wooden ball along the ground. It was half the size of him, at least.

"This is a walking globe," he said, sounding proud. "Me and Polly spotted it a few weeks ago, down in some ditch. And we hid it back here."

This ball really didn't look very special. "What does it do?" I asked.

Larkin rolled it into the centre of the ring and then stood up, puffing hard. "It don't *do* anything. You walk on it."

I smirked. "Is that all?"

"When was the last time you tried balancing *and* moving at the same time on something completely round?"

Alma came over and smoothed her hands over the wood. "Show us then."

"I will." With a hand on Alma's shoulder, Larkin climbed on to the ball. He steadied himself and Alma and I stepped back to watch.

He propelled the ball forward, moving very fast with his arms out. His feet flapped over each other, taking tiny steps, until they were practically a blur. By sharply twisting the top of his body, he moved the ball around, changing direction. It was quite something.

"I want to juggle knives at the same time, but can't manage that yet."

He suddenly wobbled and thrust his arms out for balance, but his feet were out of rhythm. I was too far back to be able to reach him before he pinwheeled backwards and thudded to the ground. Thank goodness the ground was so packed with sawdust.

"You all right?" Alma shouted. We rushed over to him. He rolled around in anguish, clutching his ankle.

"Now you've gone and done it!" I scolded.

Alma knelt over him and gently prodded his legs. "Where does it hurt?" She pressed his thigh and he shook his head. His eyes were closed and his lips pressed together. When she pushed against his shin and calf, he winced, but only a little. Her fingers moved over to lightly grip his ankle and he howled, slapping her hand away.

"No bone has pierced the skin," she said, clearly relieved. "That's good. Perhaps . . . a sprain?"

I turned away, queasy, but Alma clenched her jaw and pushed her sleeves up. Larkin's ankle was twisted. The skin around it had puffed up and turned purple, almost in front of our very eyes.

"You need to help," she said to me, firmly. "The foot must be moved back to its normal position, as much as it can be. Least till a doctor can be called. Ted, see if there's any starch, or glue bandages."

"Glue what? How do you know this?" I asked, amazed.

"My sister did similar once – jumping across the workhouse beds. She spent a night with nothing but bread and water for that. In the mornin' her ankle was the size of a ball! But I fixed up hers and I can fix up Larkin now, too."

"I can't perform like . . . how will I be . . .?" Larkin's

eyes fluttered closed. He'd gone a grey, ashy colour.

"The bruised parts should be in a pail of water, and pressed gently with someone's hand or a soft cloth for ten minutes or longer when it's this bad. Ted, go and fetch help!"

She turned back towards Larkin, who was whimpering. "Larkin, hush now! Ted, go!"

21.

Pablo had ridden for a doctor, who came to set Larkin's ankle. He praised Alma for her quick thinking and told Larkin he needed to elevate his leg and be off it for at least a week. There was nothing further to be done; it would only heal if pressure was kept off it.

Polly and Alma had created an area in the sleeping tent and fixed it so that when the opening flap was pinned back Larkin had a clear view across the field, between the wagons, and could see everything, so that he wouldn't miss too much.

Pablo had asked me to keep an eye out. 'That boy doesn't hold with idleness,' he told me.

I poked my head inside the tent after the afternoon performance, not sure how I'd be received. He'd been in and out of sleep for much of the day so far.

I sat on the chest beside his makeshift bed. "Do you have something to read?"

"I can't read." Larkin shrugged. "Used to be able to. Before chimneys, before they – my folks – got sick, I went to a dame school. It was all right, too. But after I was on my own . . . well, feeding myself became more important than learnin' my letters."

"I could teach you, if you like. I taught George a little, before. . ." I trailed off and wondered if George had gotten any further with learning his words. I hoped he hadn't given up.

"What do I need to read for anyways?" Larkin mumbled.

"You might get bored, and you've got to rest, the doctor said, so what else have you to do?"

"Thought I'd spend most of it laughing at you."

I batted him lightly on the arm. "Haha, you ought to be a clown."

He grinned. "Yeah, I been thinking that myself. All right, what's there to read?"

I rummaged in my cloth sack – I had just the thing.

"This." I pulled my *Varney the Vampire* pamphlet out. Larkin's eyes widened in delight – or fright – as he took it from me, staring at the cover. The picture *was* quite shocking: a half-skeletal figure ready to pounce on a sleeping woman.

"How graves give up their dead. . ." I whispered,

spookily. Larkin nearly leapt up, though of course he couldn't.

He opened the pamphlet and stared at the pictures, mouth half open. "Go on then – show me. Read!"

Later, I passed the Bellini brothers, practising like always, and waved at Clara, Alma and Polly, all sat on the steps of Pablo's wagon, costumes and spangles spread over their laps, getting ready for the evening performance.

I wandered down the field, not thinking of anything much, when I noticed the rope tied between two trees. It wasn't too high off the ground, probably about knee height. Larkin often strung up a low tightrope wherever we pitched up. I'd seen him walk across it, fall off, get back on.

I've no idea why I did what I did next. I don't know if I was curious or just bored, but suddenly it seemed important that I try and stand on that rope.

I eased my boots off. The field was empty, quiet. I fetched two crates so that I'd be able to reach the rope.

I wriggled my toes, feeling the cool grass. Wrapping an arm around the tree trunk and – *put your right foot up on to the rope, your body should be over the rope and then you push off with your left foot and get on* – I pulled myself on to the rope.

173

I stood, stiffly, trying to remember what I'd heard Larkin and Pablo say when they discussed ropewalking techniques.

Point my toes, don't lean forward, and keep straight. Find somewhere in the distance to focus on; something to stare at will help.

Then those thoughts and all that effort just ... vanished and blue sky swarmed into my mind and filled it. I looked ahead to the other tree trunk and a stillness swallowed me up.

Calmly, I slid my foot forward, then my other foot; I slipped and hugged the rope with the arch of my foot, which curled round it as easily as if I grasped a pole in my hand. I held my arms out to the sides, as I had watched Larkin do, but that felt like I might topple, so I raised them above my head, loosely, as if I were waving.

And I walked.

I walked and I wobbled and I walked.

Me! Walking the tightrope!

I lost my balance after three steps. Jumped down before I fell. Climbed up on those crates and tried again. Fell. Jumped. Climbed. Got to halfway.

On the twelfth attempt, I pictured waltzing round my kitchen with Mother, for no other reason than we'd had a good day.

I walked out into the middle of the rope and it was no different than walking on the ground.

Everything inside me quietened and settled. I wasn't wobbling, and I wasn't scared. I walked slowly along.

This was it!

I suddenly knew, with absolute certainty, that I would be able to dash from one end to the other, if I chose to. I reached the other tree, barely aware I'd even moved, and I laid my hand against the damp moss, springy under my palm. A tiny green shoot tickled my fingertips.

I could do this all day.

I bounced a little and the rope swayed with me. I don't know how I did it, because I wasn't thinking too hard, but I turned and walked straight back to the other tree, the way I'd come. Once I'd reached it, I jumped down on to the grass, a grin almost splitting my face.

I wanted to sing and shout and laugh, but I squidged those feelings up into a ball instead where they roiled warm around my stomach. Satisfaction spread through my entire body, until it may as well have set my fingertips glowing.

I can do something. Me. Ted Fanque can really do something!

Suddenly, all the joy vanished and I shivered as reality settled over me. I'd better practise. Maybe this could be my chance. My chance to really make a difference. Larkin wouldn't be able to perform with his injured ankle, and with no extra funds to hire a walker, Pablo couldn't afford to cancel any shows.

I needed to do this for us all. I had to get this right.

"Hey, I been looking for you. What you doing?"

I turned round to see Alma.

"Don't worry, it's not too high."

"I ain't worried – you're barely off the ground. Although we don't need anyone else injured round here now, do we?"

There was nothing to say to that, except: "I shan't fall!"

"How do you know?"

Alma was turning into a right little lady; Polly's influence was rubbing off on her, and perhaps Larkin's was rubbing off on me too, because I grinned impishly and said, "I just . . . *do*."

All I thought about was placing one foot in front of the other; it was taxing to explain, unless she was up there with me. Every time I inched forward, I thought of how Pablo must have felt, up so high when he was my age, and how Mother felt too, balancing on her first horse.

Putting one foot cautiously in front of the other is all any of us can do, isn't it? In life, in everything. There isn't much point worrying about what went before, or what might come after, because none of us can control anything, except what we're doing right *now*.

Try and do our best, and no more.

So, I walked for Alma to see. Slowly and carefully and respectfully across the rope without stopping once, jumping down when I reached the other end.

Alma's mouth hung half open, a flash of green cabbage stuck between the gap in her front teeth.

This was it! I had found my talent. Here was something I could do. Who would have thought I'd feel as at home in the air as I was on the ground?

My heart had become a balloon and was floating up into the sky.

22.

Larkin placed a wooden pole along the ground, as thick as a broom handle and not much longer. He pointed to it. "Get your boots off."

I sat on the bench and did as I was told.

"You want to try and walk rope? Even if you have natural ability, it won't harm to learn how the rest of us do it. We might have some tips. You need to get the pole right between your first and second toes, all right? Try and spread them, to get a grip, see?" Larkin wiggled the toes of his uninjured foot. They spread apart as easily as if they were his fingers.

"The middle of your heel, balance that at the back of the pole. Then, slide your other foot along your ankle a bit before moving it forward. Keep your knees slightly bent and your arms overhead, wrists loose."

I did exactly as he said and tried to grip the pole, although my toes wouldn't open wide enough. The bones strained in my feet. "It hurts!" I cried. It felt unnatural – this was harder than the actual rope!

Larkin flipped through *Varney* and said, "Toughen up! Your feet have been too protected. The skin is soft and useless. You need heels as hard as rock. That means your feet will be strong, and you'll be less likely to get injured once you're jumping and landing, see?"

I swallowed the ball of fear, like cold porridge, and stepped on to the pole again. Already, my toes and heel flexed, feeling for the familiarity; it struck me that our bodies were much cleverer than our minds sometimes.

"Where do I look then, when I'm walking along?"

"At the crowd. Give them what they've come to see. Bow and wave and smile. Even if your stomach is flopping inside-out, never show it. Whether you're learning on the pole up high, or down low, it's the same act of balancing. Eventually you'll be jumping. Got it?"

"Got it." And I really did.

I knocked on the door of Pablo's wagon. I was springy, on my tiptoes, wanting to show him what I could do, that *finally* I could do something, but also apprehensive in case I was deluding myself.

"Come in!" he said.

I stepped inside the small space. Pablo was hunched over his bunk, buttoning up his waistcoat. He looked up at me, started to speak and then stopped.

I waited. He obviously had something on his mind.

He said quietly, "Maybe I was wrong in taking you away from your mother and George in such a fashion. I wasn't thinking."

He gazed at the floor, shoulders slumped. "I *was* thinking, but perhaps wasn't focused on what I should have been. I was selfish. I thought you were like me; that you'd be excited for this life, but I can see you've no affinity with the horses. And that's all right, Ted. I certainly can't ... force you. Wouldn't commit you to a life you derived no pleasure from.

"Some might say a child should do their father's bidding, but growing up how I did, I believe choice is vital. If I can give you a little of that ... choice ... then I can still be proud."

Although it was rude to interrupt, I was bursting to tell him he had no need to feel penitent for bringing me here.

"It's *me* who ought to apologize, sir. From the moment I saw you in our living room, I'd already made up my mind to dislike the circus. I haven't made much effort." I cleared my throat, scarcely believing these words spilling from my lips, but it felt good speaking the truth.

"I didn't want to leave my life behind, but I see

now how *different* life can be. I came here to say . . . I'll never be a rider like you, or Mother, that the horses aren't for me, but I *have* found something, something which thrills me, and if you please, if you've time now, sir, *Father*, then I'd like to show you."

He shook his head, not disagreeing, but as if his mind was elsewhere. "Pablo's Family Circus isn't in a good place, Ted." His voice dropped low. "This time, I might – I might actually . . . be *finished*."

Had I heard correctly?

His face clouded over. "No one's been paid for weeks. The hired-in acts refuse to come back. I never set out to deliberately deceive anyone, but I'm running out of goodwill. I just . . . I'm not too clever with money. I should have written everything down, kept better accounts, and realized sooner that not everyone in business is a gentleman, or honourable, no matter how silver their tongues may be."

"What do you mean?"

"I'm in debt, Ted. I have no assets, nothing of value. My foolish actions! If only I hadn't been so concerned with . . . proving myself. Perhaps I could have held on to things a little longer. But, without an auspicious start in life, sometimes I needed to do more than most.

"And I admit, I relished being at the top. Riding

round these parts, people waved and cheered my name. *They knew who I was.* The colour of my skin or where I'd come from didn't matter. But now I've been forced to sell my *own circus* and rent it back from Batty; I'm so ashamed that I've told no one. I hoped to build a legacy for you and your brothers. I just wish there was . . . *more.* More time. More shows."

He put his head in his hands. His skin looked ashen. "I thought horses and the high wire would be majestic enough, but bigger circuses have lions and tigers and seal cubs and elephants! I cannot compete with all this . . . *progress.*"

Pablo couldn't look me in the eye. I'm not sure if I had grown, or he had shrunk, but I found myself putting my hand on his shoulder.

"I think what you've built is wonderful, Father. The Stockport show is in a week. Will you help me make my act something to remember?"

He met my gaze and smiled, his eyes cheerful once again. "Larkin finally get you up on a horse?"

I shook my head. "Come and see. We'll make the Stockport show a success, I promise. But then, afterwards, perhaps . . . it's time to consider something else."

"I'm not sure I know how to do anything else."

"You'll find something. And whatever it is, you'll

do your best. Because . . . that's what us Darby men do, isn't it?"

Pablo's smile was small, but it was there. "Us Fanque men, you mean."

23.

Brown had fashioned a piece of wood that Alma had found into a makeshift crutch for Larkin to hobble around on. It had been three days since his fall. His ankle wasn't too painful, now he'd taken to supping beer to help him sleep, he reminded us. The way Polly waited on him, he was almost enjoying himself.

And maybe it was the fact that I'd offered to step up, or the fact that Pablo had told Larkin what a valued member of the troupe he was, I'm not sure – maybe he was just grateful I'd introduced him to *Varney the Vampire* – but Larkin was as mellow and agreeable as I'd ever known him.

We had four days before the big Stockport show. Pablo said that newspapermen were coming to review it. Larkin lay on a heap of straw, fashioned into a bed, yelling instructions up to me. We were in the big tent, practising using the real rope, though not as high as it would be on the actual night.

"As long as you focus, you'll be able to do this."

"A little rope between two trees is one thing, but this is quite another! How do I actually stay up?"

"Shift most of your weight over the part of your body that's holding you up. If you feel unbalanced, grasp the rope between your big toe and the second one. But the crowd will be watching, and no one's impressed if you grip the rope between your toes, so try not to. Want to try using a balance bar?"

I crossed the rope slowly and back again. "Why?"

"A balance bar can make it easier to cross the rope, though many of us think using one is a cheat. Keep your centre directly over the rope though because you don't want to rock."

Pablo called up. "Keep yourself centred! Think. You're like an inverted pyramid . . . a bar would help you. It would take more to knock you off balance."

"But it's easier with my hands above my head!" I cried down to them. I stepped forward and sent a vibration along the rope and then back.

"Keep moving! A misstep or slip will mean you need to readjust, that's all."

This is how we spent two days: Pablo and Larkin yelling tips and me going further on the big rope in the tent with each practice session.

*

Back on the road, we headed for Stockport – our biggest show yet. As our wagons paraded through the streets, I sat up front for the first time, smiling and waving, along with Larkin. Alma and Polly were behind us and I felt the buzz that Larkin often spoke of, of all eyes upon us, longing to be a part of what we were offering. I hadn't noticed before – I'd been too busy wondering what Mother and George were doing. If only Mother and George could be here to see me now though!

Children ran alongside us until the roads grew too narrow and the hedges too thick and then it was only our wagons banging by, until we arrived at more rows of houses with new sets of eager faces peering out of doorways.

Then it became busier. I had forgotten what a usual day in a market town was like. We paraded through town, wagon wheels rattling over the stones; top-hatted gentlemen and bell-skirted ladies weaved in and out of the gigs and two-wheeled hansoms roared by. Such din!

It was nearly impossible to imagine that in only a few hours I'd be up on the rope with an audience watching every move I made. Me, Ted Darby, Ted *Fanque* – showing an audience that I was my father's son!

I breathed in deeply as we passed an open window: mutton pie. Contented, I watched street sellers offering fruit and a girl selling lavender and herbs. A man with poles strung with rabbits, hanging off his shoulders, walked by. A ringing bell announced a man with a tray on his head bearing muffins.

We were in the heart of town and the community. Next to the Rose and Crown, we turned in and settled on the land belonging to an old friend of Pablo's. Often the fields we arrived at were away from streets and houses, on the outskirts of town, but here, everyone could see us. Already a crowd of children, excited and curious, hung around the fences, admiring the horses.

A thrill ran up my legs and tingled in my tummy as I proudly helped unload.

I was a part of things now. I knew what we were doing, and where things went. Enthusiastic faces watched the troupe: Larkin and Alma, Polly, Clara, the Bellini brothers and Brown all working as a team. It felt good. No, more than that, it felt *great*.

Alma crept in behind the curtain before I was due to go on for my performance. Grinning ear to ear, she asked, her eyes sparkling, "You all right?"

I nodded. "I think so," I whispered.

"All the practice you done now, I ain't never seen you fall."

"It *is* much higher."

"Pablo's made it safe. He's put down mattresses. Loads of 'em. While you was kipping, he was out all afternoon: him, Brown and the Bellinis, knocking on doors. They know folks round here. They've covered them up, so they can't be seen, but mattresses *are* there and will cushion your fall if you . . . slip. Go and do your very best." She clapped her hands together excitedly. "I can't wait to have another orange!"

24.

As I dragged the curtain back, it felt heavier than a sack of flour. I walked across the sawdust ring, just behind Brown, who was rolling around, singing a Shakespearean song.

I climbed up the ladder attached to the masts that held up the circus tent. The audience were now quiet. I looked across the abyss, to where I had to reach the other wooden platform. The rope stretched between – my road in the sky.

Even though Larkin's training and Pablo's reassurance echoed round my head, my body had its own ideas. I was tight with fear, every muscle twitching and tense.

Pablo's voice came to me, distant, as if from a dream, and I heard flute music too, like the tune I'd dreamt of when I first arrived.

Pablo gazed up at me, and straightened his grey

coat, braided with black, ornamented with a gold chain hanging from the breast pocket to one of the buttonholes. He doffed his low-crowned hat and gave a flourish with his arm, as he announced:

"And now, ladies and gentleman, boys and girls ... please, welcome my son ... *the Wondrous Walker Ted Fanque!*"

I hadn't thought it would be silent, up so high, but I heard nothing. I waited for the pounding rush of blood in my ears to settle, and it did, eventually, like always.

I could do this. I was born for it.

The world dropped away. I glanced down, comforted by the lumpy sawdust beneath me. I was at least three giraffes high off the ground. I wanted a moment to fix this scene in my mind, but then, below me, on the front benches, I squinted, recognizing two faces.

My heart beat faster, not with fear, but with excitement. I steadied my breath. Mother and George! They clutched each other's arms, looking more nervous than I felt. Mother gave a huge smile. I blinked away happy tears.

And...

... I stepped out. *Hush.* The rope felt like a friend cradling me. I walked out into the centre, slowly, carefully, with my head held high, trying to make my arms flow gracefully. I stopped and balanced on one leg and then the other. When I reached the end, I crossed again. I stood in the middle and bowed, waving at the crowd. They cheered so loud.

All those shocked and smiling faces. Each collective sharp intake of breath reminded me of how candlewicks lick to life once lit.

Afterwards, behind the curtain, I trembled, buzzing with adrenaline. The back tent flapped, and I turned around: Mother and George. I rushed into Mother's outstretched arms. I'd been with the circus six weeks, but in many ways it had felt like a lifetime.

Mother squeezed me tight. I pressed my cheek against her shawl, feeling the soft wool. After a while, she held me away from her, at arm's length.

"I never had any idea you could do that!" she said, almost breathless, looking at me in wonder.

"Nor did I!" I laughed, tears of joy swimming into my eyes.

"You've grown." George stepped forward and patted me on the shoulder. "You'll be as tall as me one of these days, eh?" His cough had all but gone and he had a good colour in his cheeks.

I puffed myself up and said, "I am already!"

Together, the three of us walked across the circus

ground, weaving in between crowds. The evening's performance was still happening, but Mother, George and I were content being together, exchanging our news, in our own little bubble.

"Oranges." Mother stopped walking to sniff the air deeply. "I miss this life," she said, softly. "The excitement of performing."

"Do you?" I asked, surprised. "You never spoke of it."

"Your grandparents never approved," she admitted. "I was young and only wished to please them, but now ... well, yes, I *do* miss it. I believed that once I became a mother I should settle down. Live a more..." she sighed and shook her head. "I'm not certain. A more conventional life, perhaps? The circus life isn't an easy one, certainly. I've seen tents destroyed by fire and the weight of unmelted snow rip through canvases; I've gone a week with two hours' sleep a night and have known empty houses." She paused and looked up at the sky before smiling. "But, I've also known houses so packed that people had to stand six deep round the doors.

"When my mother needed me at the pub, going home seemed ... prudent. Every so often I'd return to help Pablo, if he happened to be touring nearby. When you boys were tiny, you came along with me. But when you fell off a pony once, Ted, you became hysterical around horses. Then the Bradfield flood happened. Sometimes in this life, you must set aside your own desires for the good of others, but not a day goes by that I don't think of my time with the circus."

For the first time, I clearly saw that underneath the crinoline and buttoned-up-ness was a horse rider and adventurer − not just my mother − missing a life she had loved dearly. She'd given it up in order to offer us a different life.

The three of us stood by the cooking pot and supped tea, watching the crowds file out of the big tent as the performance ended.

"Do you think you'd like to come back to the circus?" I asked.

Mother's eyes widened, but before she could reply, Pablo was behind her, nuzzling her cheek.

He beamed at me. "What a triumph you were, Ted! It was like seeing myself up there."

"You've done a fine job, William," my mother said. "I'm glad you persuaded me it was the right time."

Pablo's voice was soft, and he looked at her steadily. "And have you yet decided whether it is the right time for us now too?"

On the heels of Pablo, Alma sprinted towards us, jabbering with excitement, closely followed by a half-hopping, half-skipping Larkin with his crutch.

"Good job! And next time, we'll have you sitting down in the middle of the act," Larkin announced, clapping his hand on my back.

"I'm surprised I got across at all," I stammered. "Thank goodness for those mattresses."

"Mattresses?" Pablo raised his eyebrows.

Larkin echoed him, wrinkling his face. "What mattresses?"

Alma winked at me. "Anyone for tea?" she grinned.

There we were, the six of us, gazing back towards the big tent, across the circus ground.

And I knew, with the same certainty that day follows night, that whatever difficulties came our way, we'd muddle through together. None of us were perfect, but, just like the parts of my beloved kaleidoscope, depending on how you looked at it and how the light filtered in, we could fit together to make the commonplace unique and our lives sublime.

This was my circus family.

Author's Note

Pablo Fanque first came to my attention through a writer friend of mine. I'd never heard of him before, though his story certainly sparked my imagination.

When the opportunity to write for the *Voices* series came my way, knowing I was interested in the Victorian period, it was a wonderful melding of ideas, because Pablo's circus and his family were around during those times. I knew immediately that I wanted to work with them somehow.

I've long been a fan of the circus and fairgrounds. I believe they offer not only an escape from the 'everyday', but also offer us a glimpse into an alternative world, as close to magic as we'll ever witness.

Having read about Pablo, and the life he'd had, and then reading about his sons, all the elements were there, it seemed, to create a fascinating story.

I have a lot in common with Ted, and that made it

easy and essential to find his voice and to be able to tell his story. I have never met my own father, and around the same age as Ted, I grew up in a small village and was the only mixed-race person in my entire primary school! I understood and empathised with his feelings of difference and could imagine how it might have felt back then.

In writing about people based on real historical figures, the writer has a tricky arena to negotiate. We need to engage our imagination, whilst trying to remain faithful to the source material and any research we've unearthed. But, it's long been my favourite activity to base stories on real people in history. To put myself in their shoes and imagine how they must have felt, depending on their circumstances.

I hope that I've done Pablo, Ted, George and Elizabeth justice. Studying their lives and the lives of circus folk in Britain in the 1800s for the past nine months, I've certainly felt their presence strongly. Although over one hundred and fifty years separates us from them, I believe that the qualities of determination, commitment and dignity they demonstrated can still be appreciated today.

I'd like to end by telling you a real-life snippet I discovered, during my research, about the older Ted Fanque.

He wrote to the newspaper the *World's Fair* on

28 November 1914, protesting about not being allowed to fight in the war. Because he was over forty-five, even though he was fit and healthy, he'd been deemed 'too old to fight', but he lobbied for all those older men who wished to fight to put their names forward.

I believe that demonstrates the type of man Ted grew up to become. He was willing to stand up for what he believed in and to campaign to try and make a change when he could.

I do hope you enjoy reading about these wonderful people as much as I enjoyed writing about them. I miss them already.

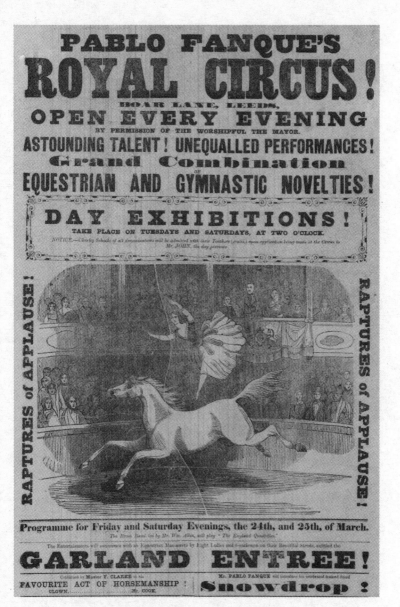

Reproduced courtesy of Leeds Library and Information Service